I0667876

The Swimmer

Other Books by
Laury A. Egan

FICTION

Jenny Kidd

Fog and Other Stories

The Outcast Oracle

Fabulous! An Opera Buffa

A Bittersweet Tale

The Ungodly Hour

POETRY

Snow, Shadows, a Stranger

Beneath the Lion's Paw

The Sea & Beyond

Presence & Absence

The *Swimmer*

A NOVEL

~

LAURY A. EGAN

Heliotrope Books
New York

Copyright © 2021 Laury A. Egan

All rights reserved. No part of this book may be reproduced or transmitted in any form or by any means, electronic or mechanical, including photocopying, recording or by an information storage or retrieval system now known or heretoafter invented—except by a reviewer who may quote brief passages in a review to be printed in a magazine or newspaper—without permission in writing from the publisher: heliotropebooks@gmail.com

This is a work of fiction. Names, characters, places, and incidents either are products of the author's imagination or are used fictitiously. Any resemblance to actual events or persons, living or dead, is coincidental.

ISBN: 978-1-942762-72-0

Copy edited by Beverly Jean Harris
Cover design by Laury A. Egan
Cover photograph by Angela Previte
Typeset Design by Heliotrope Books

PREFACE

This a work of fiction. Although care was taken, I am not a medical professional and cannot guarantee complete accuracy regarding surgical procedures, drug and chemo treatments, or other practices mentioned in the book, which were derived from research conducted before 2015 and based primarily on one patient's history. Because each person's regimen is individually tailored and their physical responses differ, the descriptions within may not portray the experience of others or reflect current protocols developed during the ensuing years. Hopefully, effective means to battle pancreatic cancer have improved, with more dramatic breakthroughs on the near horizon. To donate or for more information: www.pancan.org

1

~~~

I climbed the massive yellow dune, grateful for the breeze, though it did little to alleviate the ninety-degree heat that had been bear-hugging the northeast during the last two weeks of August. At the dune's crest, I stood, breathing heavily, legs shaking, yet triumphant.

"You won't find me here!" I declared.

No one would. I was just outside of Provincetown, the farthest I could journey out to sea without leaving land. And a place my husband wouldn't think to look for me. I'd driven here alone, to make some critical decisions about my life and its ending. When would I die and how? Would it happen soon? In weeks or months? Or would I be granted another year?

I slid down the sandy incline to the wide beach, whose tan ribbon was dotted with a few sunbathers, none of whom noticed me. The great splendor of the Atlantic Ocean unfurled before my eyes, and a crowd of cumulus clouds drifted eastward in the blue sky. I selected a spot apart from the other beachgoers, spread a pink-and-white-striped towel on the sand, and unfolded a chair into which I collapsed, winded from my exertion. Taking deep breaths of tart salt air, I tried to moderate my fast heartbeat and quiet my thoughts. Although some sixty-two-year-old women were occasionally apprehensive, my thoughts frequently churned with anxiety. Many times a day, a barrage of signals—such as pain and fatigue—reminded me that I was engaged in a lethal war. On some mornings, I was exhausted and slow to rise from bed. Often, I felt the knife-edge of fear against my throat or the ponderous weight of sadness dragging my spirit. Or I suffered as if plagued by a strange tropical fever, with thoughts that floated deliriously, refusing to congeal into any rational, cohesive organization. At those moments—such as now—I allowed myself to flow with the miasmic confusion rather than force my mind into its usual disciplined patterns.

As if in a trance, I stared at the clouds and drifted with them, admiring their graceful demise. They were almost like balloons, slowly losing buoyancy, shape, and color until they vanished. How admirable to ebb away without drama or distress! I desired that for myself and for all those suffering from terminal illnesses.

No one promises how long I will live. Thirty months ago, four doctors said that I would be dead within six months to a year from pancreatic cancer that had metastasized into my liver. *Bess, Get your life in order*, they warned. Although I have dutifully attempted to do so, I haven't been completely successful, which is why I've made this unscheduled trip as a spiritual sabbatical and a last-act referendum. Regardless of what I decide, all of my plans are necessarily short-term, even if I am a "Superior Responder," as my oncologist, Dr. Melbourne, told me last May, before my thirty-third chemo treatment. This struck me as mordantly funny because I'm a psychotherapist and listening and responding are two skills that I've diligently improved over the span of my career. The doctor noted my peculiar expression but, as usual, made no comment about my prognosis because Dr. Melbourne hasn't any clue what it is.

I stopped this internal dialogue, reminding myself that it does no good to obsess, and turned my attention to the waves. I watched each one gather itself, thrust upward to its highest pinnacle, then hang in the air before rolling over and sliding onto the flat apron of sand. Some were sharply cut at top; some were laced with gold and white chains spewed from the backwash of the breaker before it; others were small and squeezed between a series of choppy furrows. The rush and crash of the ocean soothed me and blended seamlessly with the sighing breeze. Overhead, a gull cried out, perturbed about something, and the noon sun was high and strong, doing its best to burn my chemo-sensitive skin despite the sunscreen I had applied.

Into this reverie, my cell phone intruded. Although I didn't want to speak with anyone and had closed my practice, a few clients needed help on occasion; help that was restricted to phone sessions and only when I felt well enough.

The caller was Hugh Chatham, my husband. He'd left four messages already, each of which probably contained exclamatory comments. My son, Nathan, and my best friend, Susan Collier, had also telephoned, but it was Hugh on the line now. He needed an explanation about why I'd departed so abruptly, leaving only a terse note to say I was traveling alone for a few days. I hadn't mentioned my destination.

"Hello, Hugh."

"Where are you?"

"I'm where I should be, where I wish to be."

"Good god, Elizabeth, that doesn't answer my question! What's the matter? Are you all right?" He sounded annoyed, probably because Hugh wasn't accustomed to fending for himself.

"I'm fine."

Hugh only uses my full name, Elizabeth, when he believes his paternal forbearance or a little gentle chiding is necessary. For a moment, he was silent, probably recalling that I wasn't well and therefore, in his mind, not fully responsible for my actions. Of course, it was also likely that he was troubled by my failure to be clear and communicative, which I ordinarily was, thus allowing Hugh the luxury of being vague and withholding—our longstanding marital dynamic.

"It's just that I…I don't know where you are," he stammered.

I didn't reply. I felt the familiar ache in my back and altered my position in the chair. As on numerous occasions, I wondered if Hugh had precipitated my cancer. This was nonsense, but nevertheless I harbored a small belief that this was true. At the least, my anger toward him had become a fiery nugget, not unlike the tumors that were making a meal of my pancreas.

"Really, Bess, I know you're upset and not yourself, but you just can't go off without telling me."

"Why not?"

Hugh snorted with disapproval. "Because, my dear, I could have rearranged my schedule and come with you."

"I didn't want that."

I pictured him tucking in his chin, which was punctuated by a deep cleft. When we first met, I'd thought that the indentation, matched by dimples in his cheeks, made him appear dashing. As he had aged, Hugh's face had become lined and fleshy; by now, at sixty-nine, jowls had formed, making him look more distinguished than handsome.

"Well, I worry about you. You know I do."

While he might worry some, he hadn't worried enough over the decades before I fell ill and hadn't worried sufficiently since. It was tempting to tell him this, to lay a mile-long list of grievances at his feet, but accusation was not my habit. Still, something in me had changed. This shift became more pronounced as we spoke.

"I'll return when I feel like it, Hugh. I need to spend time by myself."

"I see." He seemed more mystified than defeated by my behavior. "How long will you be away?"

"I'm not sure. As long as I am."

"Bess, that's not a proper answer! What should I do about grocery shopping and…dinner?"

I laughed at him. "Order take-out or go to a restaurant. Besides, you can cook."

"But Bess!"

I let my irritation color my words. "Hugh, you're not a child. You can take care of yourself."

He expelled a gust of air. "Will you call me when you're in a better mood? This evening? And explain?"

Hugh's voice, which I once admired for its mellifluousness, had become grating. His chauvinistic insinuation that I was behaving like an emotional female, that he would patiently wait for me to return to my senses, was insulting, as was his forbearance—manufactured to appear sincere, yet the effort to do so was thinly concealed. My feelings, already hardened against him, hardened even more.

Whenever I disagree with someone, I usually couch my words with softening phrases to deter confrontation. I felt no such diplomatic impulse now. For many years, I had also disguised my frustration with my husband, waiting for it to dissipate. It hadn't.

"I'm sorry, Hugh. I won't telephone tonight."

The abrupt firmness stunned him into silence. I waited a few seconds and then disconnected, without saying goodbye.

I couldn't remember doing this to Hugh before. I imagined him standing near the black leather sofa in our book-lined living room, with its Chinese red walls and floral green and gold draperies. He would place his cell phone in the inside breast pocket of his jacket and frown. His eyes might narrow, and the creases on his forehead might deepen. Or perhaps my behavior would totally surprise him. Maybe Hugh was thrusting his fingers through his long silver hair to console himself for having such an unfathomable wife or was staring at the flowers in the crystal vase on the coffee table. As usual, he wouldn't really see them, as he had rarely seen me.

I realized I didn't care how Hugh felt, which was astonishing after thirty-seven years of marriage.

"Does this mean you're done?" I asked myself.

The gray and white seagull returned, his raspy cry ripping the air and bringing me back to a gentler memory. Of Nathan's first trip to the beach when he had struggled to balance on his fat, bowed legs and half-ran, half-crawled after a seagull, who was perched on a nearby log. Hugh had gathered Nathan in his arms and rushed at the bird, who flew away. This delighted Nathan and he clapped his hands, grinning merrily. A lovely time, one of many Hugh and I shared. However, our marriage had begun to splinter even before our son's birth, the discord due to one issue: my husband was a serial philanderer.

When we were newly married, I was twenty-five and deeply in love with Hugh. I had made a commitment to him as he had to me. When I found out about the first affair, I didn't know what to do and, foolishly, did nothing decisive. From then on, it became difficult to give myself freely to Hugh, with trust and passion. We had sex—sometimes it was exciting and satisfying—but my knowledge of his deceit tainted our intimacy. To avoid romantic moments, I retreated into my private practice, working more evening hours and feigning tiredness when I came home. Ironically, while I established a safe haven for my clients, I was also creating a safe place for myself, where I concentrated on other people's problems and not my own.

Hugh, a philosophy professor, fashioned his own withdrawal, delving into arcane texts to support his academic publications and climbing all the rungs of his department until he had become the chairman. During our early years together, I believed that Hugh's work was important, a fascinating exercise of the mind, until I saw how his studies allowed him to subsist in the lofty provinces of thought—in a dead, cool, abstract refuge so different from the alive, warm, and human place I inhabited. And, too, his work provided an excuse for late-night trysts and weekend visits to university libraries accompanied by fetching grad students or pretty associate professors.

I grasped a broken clamshell and used its rounded edge to smooth the hill of sand beside me. During my childhood, when my family lived on the northern coast of New Jersey, I had dreamed of having a home or office with large windows where I could gaze upon the ocean. Instead, just before our marriage, I agreed to move inland, to a house in Stamford, so Hugh could bicycle to the university. Unfortunately, this first capitulation became one of many, though I later began protesting more often.

His relationships also continued, most of which he denied. Even when I produced evidence of his infidelity, he acted as if his sexual transgressions should pass by without causing a ripple in the sea of matrimony. Over the years, I almost stopped objecting, as, one by one, women flamed in his heart, consumed his attention until their appeal diminished, and the relationship turned to cold ash and blew away.

"You enabled him," I muttered. "Exactly what you counsel your clients not to do."

The word "hypocrite" pinned its hot brand on my forehead. I removed my straw hat and fanned myself to dissipate the heat. Even after my cancer diagnosis, Hugh kept having sporadic affairs, which were unbearably hurtful. Why hadn't I left him? Was I afraid of being alone? And why hadn't he left me?

Although we have had many happy periods, staying married to Hugh has been an uneven struggle. Two days ago, however, after seeing Dr. Melbourne—the first visit this summer because I was given a reprieve from chemo—I concluded it might be time to leave. If, under my present dire circumstances, Hugh couldn't be a consistent help or even attend my important medical appointments, then when would he ever be a true partner? I was tired of watching him veer between mouthing the right phrases and withdrawing into obtuseness.

I placed my hat on the towel and weighed its brim down with a book. After removing my white linen shirt, I came to my feet and walked toward the water, feeling the hot grainy sand mold to my arches. At the water's edge, I stepped in and enjoyed the ocean's coldness, which instantly translated upward so the rest of my body cooled. Because I was concerned about damaging the port inserted in my chest for treatment infusions and because no guard was on duty, I only ventured thigh-high into the surf, despite my lifelong passion for swimming, nor did I wish to struggle with the temptation to dive in and rush past the point of return, into oblivion.

The frothy water sluiced around me, buffeting my legs. As I

stood there, feeling euphoric in my favorite element, the hot wind from the land shifted and began blowing off the ocean, bringing with it a strange chill. I shivered, and considered a retreat to the warmth of the beach, when the breeze suddenly swiveled to its original westerly course. I thought of our neighbor's creaky wind vane and its tendency to spin without settling on a consistent direction. Hugh called it "the drunken eagle." That bird would be getting an exhaustive workout here.

I walked a few feet, trailing my hands along the water, and then noticed a man with white hair swimming parallel to the shoreline. He was about twenty yards out, where the waves begin their slow thickening, and appeared very powerful, with a physique that didn't resemble that of an older man, leading me to wonder if he dyed his hair or his hair had turned prematurely white. I watched him cross in front of me, make a neat turn, and continue in the opposite direction without a pause. After one large wave blocked him from view, I waited for the breaker to pass and sought out the swimmer once again. He was still moving fast, but behind him were two dark fins.

I gasped. My hand rose into the air. "Sharks!" I cried, pointing furiously.

The man swam for a few seconds before stopping. Because I was the only person nearby, he gave me a questioning look, then turned to his left, jerked with surprise, and headed toward shore, his strokes strong, his feet and hands making almost no splashes.

I tore out of the water, spun around, glued my eyes to Jaws and his mate, and watched them angle in menacing crisscross patterns. My hands curled into fists and my breathing quickened, as if in preparation to fight off the sharks, which, of course, I couldn't do. In what seemed like hours, the swimmer finally reached the shallows, came to his feet, and burst upward, water sliding in sheets off of his beautifully sculpted body, which gleamed like creamy white marble. When he joined me on the beach, the man brushed back short locks of white hair and observed me with blue eyes so full of sunlight that they seemed incapable of revealing an internal emotion.

"Thank you!" he said, between gulps of air. "Wow! That was a close one!" His shoulders rose and he shuddered. "Needless to say, I didn't see them."

"You're welcome. I'm glad I did."

The man might have been fifteen years younger than I am, but the more I looked at him—and it was difficult to look anywhere else—I became less sure of his age. His face was perfect in its symmetry and remarkably unlined, with a long, aquiline nose and a broad, clean forehead. Quite simply, the man was stunning.

He exhaled slowly, as if trying to quiet his agitation, and wiped water from his white eyebrows, which ran with level precision above his eyes except for a downturn at their ends.

"Oh, sorry not to introduce myself." He adjusted the white bathing trunks on his hips and extended a large hand. "Stephen Andersen."

His grasp was cool and firm. "Elizabeth Lynch. Nice to meet you."

"Elizabeth or…?"

"Bess. Whichever you prefer. And you? Steve or Stephen?"

"Stephen. Makes me sound more substantial." He laughed, his blue eyes twinkling with amusement. Then he directed his attention to the ocean and grew more serious. The two fins had vanished as suddenly as they had arrived. "Guess they found better things to eat," he said. "Even so, I don't think I'll put a toe in the water again today. Too bad!" His smile broke out a second time. Like the rest of him, his teeth were flawless. "Maybe I'll stick to swimming pools from now on!"

It was my turn to laugh. Together, we strolled upward onto the thick sand, our footprints disappearing into its small undulating hills and valleys. I kept glancing at him, wondering if I'd conjured this Adonis from the chemo-induced fog that occasionally swirled in my brain. None of the people nearby seemed to pay him any attention, which I thought astonishing, but as I scanned the ocean, I noticed no one had vacated the water, either, despite my shouted warnings.

When I reached my chair, I crossed my arms and felt another small chill regardless of the strong sun. To my surprise, Stephen placed a gentle hand on my shoulder. "You look cold."

His eyes gravitated briefly to the port on my chest. If he was familiar with its purpose, he would know I was ill.

"Yes, I am a bit." After he removed his fingers, I reached for a towel and began drying my arms before slipping on my blouse.

A bashful expression came over his face. "Hey, I don't mean to sound forward, Bess, but do you mind if I join you? I don't know anyone here…in Provincetown, I mean." He paused, then added, " And, besides, you may have just saved my life."

I smiled and nodded my head.

2

Stephen walked down the beach, grabbed a blanket and a large straw bag, and returned to where I was sitting. He stood over me, his head eclipsing the sun, his white hair illuminated like a fringed halo. I raised my hand over my eyes to block the harsh afternoon light and watched as he spread a navy wool blanket a few feet away, lowered himself onto its surface, and began rubbing his body with a towel. Although I'd come to the Cape for solitude and felt a little disconcerted to have company, I wasn't sorry to spend time with such a dazzlingly handsome man, even if I was mystified about why he would befriend me when he could have his pick of anyone. Not that I'm unattractive, but I wasn't in his league nor was I his age. I continued to gaze upon this vision of masculine perfection—his expensive haircut—longer on top, trimmed shorter below—his gym-toned body, and the fact that we were on a Provincetown beach, and came to the conclusion that Stephen was probably gay.

After he had finished drying himself, he folded his towel into a precise square, leaned back on his palms, and crossed his feet at the ankles. It was his chance to observe me as I had observed him, and he did so with curiosity melded with sensitivity. Glancing once again at the chemo port, Stephen finally focused on my face.

"So, Bess, forgive me for asking, but what brought you to Provincetown?"

"You mean why would a straight, sixty-two-year-old woman come here?" I gave him a warm smile.

Stephen nodded and looked a little sheepish. "I didn't think you were sixty-two…"

"But you do think I'm straight."

"Yeah."

"Well, thanks for saying I look younger than I am. As for orientation, I hold no prejudices whatsoever." I said this to put him at ease, in case the comment was applicable. "To answer your question, I'm visiting for a few days because I need to make some decisions." Since I didn't want to say what they were, I asked, "And you?"

Stephen studied me with unusual frankness, perhaps surmising the problems I was trying to resolve. "Like you, I have some issues to deal with."

"Important ones? Matters of life or death?"

"You might say that." He chuckled. "Although I didn't expect to have a near-death experience this afternoon."

I smiled and then let a short silence unfold between us, waiting for him to continue as I did with clients who weren't ready to reveal their thoughts. It occurred to me that Stephen might sense I was a sympathetic listener because people often commented that this quality was one of the first impressions people formed about me. Although I hadn't mentioned my profession, I hoped Stephen wasn't intuitively attracted because of my skills, yet my therapist's radar was registering traces of his sadness.

"Do you want to tell me?" I asked in a quiet voice.

Stephen looked seaward and pressed his lips together. "I don't know."

"Fair enough."

My willingness to let go of the topic surprised him. He sat up straight and folded his legs Indian-style. "And you? What are you deciding?"

I laughed. "I'm not sure I wish to talk about that now, either…"

"But you will?"

I nodded. "Maybe."

—

We spent an hour speaking about more mundane topics. I learned he lived in Boston, worked as a freelance life insurance broker, and had studied pre-med at Cornell before dropping out after his junior year, though he didn't explain why. I told Stephen about my therapeutic practice, that I had a Ph.D. in psychology and was a licensed clinical social worker, that I was recently retired. I didn't say why. We ventured into politics and world affairs, countries we had visited, but said little about our private lives. It was what I termed "cocktail party" dialogue—safe, polite, moderately informative, with outbreaks of laughter.

Although I was wearing a blouse, had donned my hat, and had covered my legs with a towel, I could feel the effects of the strong sun and could also see that Stephen's skin was becoming slightly pink.

"I think I need to get in the shade," I said, pointing at my lower forearm.

He looked down at his chest, ran his hand lightly across himself. "I'm getting a little red too." When he glanced up at me, his eyes held a question.

"So, what would you like to do?" I asked because neither of us seemed ready to end our conversation.

"I don't know," he replied. "Can I buy you a drink in town or...?"

I thought about the invitation. I didn't know Stephen well, yet I was usually a good judge of character and detected no dangerous vibes, although some sociopaths were suave and charismatic until they exhibited their true selves. Still, I was greatly enjoying Stephen's company.

"Why don't you come for dinner?" I offered. "Do you like swordfish?"

He gave me a happy grin, its brightness genuine. "I love it! What shall I bring? Some wine—if you drink wine?"

"Yes, I do. White wine." Since my diagnosis, I was allowed to

13

drink in moderation but hadn't often done so until this summer's break from treatment.

"Hmm," he said, rubbing his chin, "I bet you prefer French or Italian. And not American. Am I right?"

"Yes," I replied, a bit startled. "How did you know?"

"Ah, a lucky guess."

I gave him the address of the cottage in Truro, and Stephen explained he was staying at a motel in Provincetown and had a car. We settled on six o'clock.

—

When I entered the confines of my BMW, the heat exploded from within my body. Over the last thirty months, sudden temperature changes often scrambled my internal thermostat, making me too warm or too cold. I was now perspiring and felt dizzy. Set to full blast, the car's air conditioning helped, but as I sat there, with the windows open to dispel the hot air, I realized my energy had plummeted. This happened without warning: during house-cleaning, grocery shopping, or dinner parties. If people noticed and knew my story, they were sympathetic, yet I did my best to conceal how I felt because I'd never liked revealing personal struggles even to my family—one reason I'd just fled my home, so I could right my unbalanced ship in private. And, because being alone was necessary to do this and to resolve other crucial issues, I somewhat regretted my impromptu invitation to Stephen. Entertaining him would be a distraction, even if a pleasant one. It was also possible that I would tire during the evening and explaining about my illness to a stranger, nice as he was, was not my inclination. In fact, I'd mostly avoided heart-to-heart talks with everyone except my friend Susan. While my clients seemed to gain strength from sharing their feelings, I often felt weaker. Letting down my reserve meant allowing my defenses to crumble, leaving me without the structure that kept me upright. I'd tried to be open with Hugh, to convey the complex emotions that were flooding over me, but he usually only managed some hugs and handing me tissues when I cried. Although it was obvious he was in despair about my illness, Hugh preferred to speak about analysis and facts, his habitual method of coping.

As for Stephen, I was concerned that he was dealing with a problem and might expect our conversation to evolve into a semi-therapeutic session, a hazard I sometimes faced in social circumstances. Did I possess the fortitude for such an exchange? I wasn't sure, but I hoped that I could be present and balanced if this situation arose; yet the reverse might be true: that Stephen sensed I needed some kindness and a chance to talk. And, though I seldom sought comfort, I realized I was sorely in need of it.

Regardless of my uncertainty about dinner, the invitation couldn't be rescinded because I'd forgotten to ask for his cell phone number. I shook my head at myself, closed the windows and door, and backed out of the parking space. As the car moved forward, my spirits revived as they always did in response to the growl of the engine and the quick acceleration. I loved fast cars, cared for them dutifully, and kept each for at least ten years. Often I wondered if my attraction to speed was a reaction against my marital immobility and the stillness required by my profession—sitting in a chair for hours, listening. While driving provided an opportunity to break out of these self-imposed boxes, a new urge had recently arisen: the temptation to floor the gas pedal and drive off of a bridge or cliff, flying into space.

"Yeah, but you wouldn't want to hurt your car," I said aloud, as I headed onto Route 6. I followed this joyless remark with a second comment. "However, you could take Hugh's Volvo instead." I chuckled at that and began singing the Habanera from *Carmen*, though my recollection of the words was imperfect. It had been almost forty years since I'd studied the score, during my last years in graduate school, when I was taking voice lessons and beginning to participate in regional concerts and in one staged opera. Sadly, my talent didn't match my passion, nor was I a natural solo performer. Eventually, the demands of my fledgling therapy practice crowded music out of my schedule.

Still humming, I turned off near Truro and stopped at the fish and grocery stores. There, I purchased swordfish steaks, brown rice, Bibb lettuce, tomatoes, a loaf of French bread, two cheeses, and lobster salad for tomorrow's lunch. I then continued to Tom's Hill Road and took the narrow, sandy driveway up to the house, which sat on a rise surrounded by bayberry and scrub pines, tall oaks, and windblown sandy knolls netted with poison ivy. Wild blueberry and beach plum bushes grew in and around the small hills and land-locked dunes as did goldenrod, Queen Anne's lace, blue cornflowers, and assorted reeds and grasses. The cottage itself was a mix of old and new construction and faced with traditional cedar shingles that had aged to various shades of gray. The trim was white, the shutters black, and the brick chimney a faded red; on each side of the Dutch door, latticework trellises supported pink and white climbing roses, tenacious plants that also sprawled on split-rail fences enclosing the parking area. The building required maintenance: the gutters were sagging and choked with pine needles and the first autumn leaves, the roses needed pruning, and the humped driveway could use the attentions of a plow's blade. I didn't care. I loved the cottage.

Inside, the house was cooled by central air conditioning, a welcome relief from the humid summer heat. I entered the kitchen and placed the grocery bag on the table. Like the rooms on the two wings, the ceiling was low, with exposed wood rafters. Everything else in the cottage was painted white except the wide, honey-colored pine floorboards. Old straw baskets and copper pots hung by the door to the patio, and a bouquet of wildflowers was arranged in a green glass vase on the window sill.

After I stored all the food, I carried the vase to the dining table in the living room, whose ceiling had been raised to a story and a half. Floor-to-ceiling prow windows fronted the southeast wall, and three skylights were set in the roof. Through their generously sized plate glass, golden afternoon light brightened the room and coated the ancient oriental rugs, antique coffee table, and two armchairs. The air held the pleasant smell of sweet beach plum, which had been burned in the large fireplace, and the less pleasant remains of cigarette smoke; this odor was old and faint. The living room was friendly, lived in, and comfortable, though the owners were not the tidiest souls. Their inattentive housekeeping didn't bother me.

I walked into the bedroom, removed my blouse, shorts, and bathing suit, and tossed on some dry clothes. Grabbing my book, *Journal of a Solitude*, by May Sarton, which I thought would be an appropriate selection, I returned to the living room and sat on the sofa, whose floral-print chintz cloth was worn at the seams. Placing my hand on one of the cushions, I traced the scalloped outline of a pink rosette and followed its brownish-green stem as it tangled with an interwoven honeysuckle vine. The pattern reminded me of the wallpaper I'd chosen for my office. Comforted by the similarity, I lay down and began reading. After a few minutes, I rested the paperback on my chest and gave in to drowsiness.

———

At four-thirty, I awoke, startled, in the throes of a disturbing dream about my father, who was attempting to climb from his hospital bed, struggling with lines that snaked from his body to IV poles and various beeping monitors. He was imploring me to help, yet, for some reason, I couldn't raise myself to my feet.

I blinked my eyes, which were wet with tears, tried to catch my breath, and reiterated the standard analyst's advice, the one I gave to my clients: the characters in your dream may be who they are or they may be versions of yourself, a projection disguised by the face of a friend, lover, or parent. Using this interpretation, was my father really the central dream character? From age nine to ten, I had witnessed many similar grueling hospital scenes as he battled his illness. I had felt powerless then, but I was also powerless now, unable to evade the clutches of my own grasping disease, though chemotherapy had bought some time. Utilizing this psychological equation, my dream could depict me lying in the bed and, at the same time, sitting in the room, observing the process of my death and incapable of providing assistance; being in both roles: the enfeebled victim and the impotent onlooker.

I wiped my damp cheeks. Ever since the beginning of chemo, I'd been afflicted with hyper-realistic and distressing nightmares that persisted during the transfer from sleep to full consciousness, bleeding one state into another. I reminded myself that I was in a rental house on Cape Cod, on a comfortable couch, safe. When I finally felt more collected, I sat up and stretched. My muscles were stiff, perhaps slightly inflamed from the light sunburn, and my upper back ached; otherwise, I was refreshed. Taking afternoon naps, which I'd never done before, was now almost a daily necessity in order to counteract the debilitating effects of cancer and its treatment.

I thought about these changes, all part of my decline, which, so far, had been downhill but not precipitous, except for a scary month when I lost some hair after the third chemo. Fortunately, the shedding stopped within a few weeks, leaving my light brown hair thinner, though not visibly sparse, and intermingled with more silver strands. While I had weathered these last thirty months fairly well, I knew more challenging trials lay ahead. For these, I needed to prepare, to toughen my resolve, and to make several decisions, a major one in particular. Quiet was essential to this process, which was why I'd chosen a week-long flight from my house in Stamford.

As is sometimes the case, when a retreat is planned to con-template specific problems, those problems have already been unconsciously resolved. Looking out the window at the tawny old dunes and the stately white oaks that stood guardian around the house, I saw that my answer lay before me, clear and consolidated, separated from the morass of confusion in which it had been mired.

"Yes," I said to the room. "Yes."

Without hesitation, I reached for my cell phone.

His secretary answered on the third ring.

3

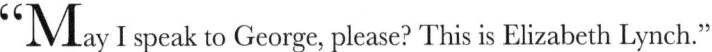

"May I speak to George, please? This is Elizabeth Lynch."

A minute passed before my attorney answered. "Bess! How are you?" His voice was cheerful, yet shaded with concern.

"I'm fine. Away for a week…a little break."

"Is Hugh with you?"

"No. That's who I'm taking a break from." I tried to sound lighthearted, but my attempt at humor was flimsy, and George's silence indicated he suspected something serious was on my mind. I lay against the sofa and looked through the large windows, watching a cardinal stitch a flight pattern between oak branches. "Actually, George, I've made a long overdue decision. I want to begin a permanent separation from Hugh."

"A divorce?"

"Yes."

"Bess, is this the right time to do this? I mean, you're going to want his help…" He drifted off, not needing to add details.

"For most people in my situation, this wouldn't make any sense. For me, it does. This falls into the category of putting my life in order."

George was acquainted with Hugh from the golf club, but he had served as my private attorney since the beginning of my marriage and was familiar with its history. Recently, I had redrawn my will, health proxy, and power-of-attorney legal documents, so George was aware that my husband had been bypassed on all three papers. Nathan had been named as my primary heir, and Susan

Collier was my designated legal and medical authority, with my son listed second, an order I might have reversed except Nathan lived almost two hours away and was dealing with a hectic life—a recently problematic relationship with his girlfriend and a very demanding job, which he was afraid of losing if he took time off.

"I see. Does Hugh know about your intentions?"

"No, he doesn't," I admitted. "And, by the way, George, I'm not at the house, but I have my laptop and there's a printer here. If you can email the documents, I'll print and sign them and return the papers overnight express."

He hesitated and then cleared his throat. "Do you have any stipulations?"

"I'd like to remain at home until I die. Afterward, as you know from my will, Nathan is to receive my share of the house, my furniture, and the items listed in the addendum. While I'm alive, I'd like everything left except for Hugh's things. And if he contests my wishes and I must move—"

"That's unlikely, Bess. I think Hugh will be considerate."

"Probably, but if he does refuse, I want to keep my personal possessions and my car—everything that I've paid for. Since we've maintained financial records from the beginning of our marriage, including for the purchase of the house and its furnishings, this should be easy to do fairly."

My pragmatic mother had advised this arrangement because I was contributing most of the house down payment, money inherited from my father. Initially, Hugh had protested this request, but he had meager savings at that point and wasn't especially interested in finances. I volunteered to keep track of our household receipts and had done so carefully.

"And alimony?" he asked.

"None. I have sufficient money. What's the point of asking for alimony given my prognosis? It's not exactly like I need a lot for my old age." After saying this, I regretted my bitter tone. "I'm sorry, George, but if you can do this quickly, I'd greatly appreciate it."

He was silent, still writing down my instructions. "All right, Bess, if you're sure." He hesitated, perhaps to give me a chance to change my mind. When I didn't speak, he added, "Everything sounds reasonable. I'll also write a letter requesting that Hugh vacate the house as part of the separation. Of course, his departure is voluntary. He's under no obligation to leave and could contest it."

"I doubt that he will."

"You're probably right. I'll start on this now. Look for the documents tomorrow morning. Once I receive them back, we'll file with the Superior Court."

I thanked my attorney and ended the call, feeling like two-hundred-fifty pounds of a six-foot-two husband had been lifted from my shoulders. However, with this divorce would come a host of problems that would dramatically increase as I became sicker. I was already using transdermal fentanyl patches regularly, though I'd skipped yesterday so I could make the journey unimpaired. That hadn't been wise. After crossing the bridge onto Cape Cod, I had pulled off the road to restore the patch because of the pain and the slight withdrawal symptoms. Dr. Melbourne had approved of my driving around Stamford unless I was tired, nauseous, or dizzy, so, barring these symptoms, which usually resolved soon, I had felt confident about making the trip. But on days when I was feeling really ill or when my condition worsened, the logistical obstacles would be significant—dealing with going to the doctor's and to chemotherapy appointments, to the stores to shop. If I lost my ability to operate a car, managing my daily life without Hugh could prove very complicated. In addition to these practical concerns, I would miss his humor and companionship, the fun we had cooking and discussing books and politics. Although I was disappointed in him, our marriage had survived because of the simple enjoyments we shared. Yet I could no longer depend on a man who wasn't dependable, a man who had left me stranded on multiple occasions, forcing me to go to chemo by myself and even cheating on me after my diagnosis. The hurt Hugh had already caused—and would cause in the future—was too much to deal with. If I possessed nothing else during my last months, I hoped to keep my integrity and whatever shreds of independence I still had. Even so, the idea of living alone was frightening.

I was also scared about the intensification in pain yesterday and today. At first, I had assumed this was due to the short fentanyl hiatus, but twenty-four hours had passed since the patch had been replaced. This led me to consider the obvious—the cancer was active again. In early June, I'd missed three chemo infusions due to a dangerous decrease in platelet levels. Because the winter and spring MRIs had shown no new tumor growth, I had been given the summer off to recuperate, but upon my return to Stamford, a new scan was scheduled. Today's sudden level of discomfort—an insistent, throbbing intrusion—was newly alarming. Had I gone too long between treatments? During our last appointment, hearing of a slight increase in pain, Dr. Melbourne had prescribed using two 50-microgram fentanyl patches instead of one, the use left to my discretion. I had filled the additional prescription and brought a twelve-day supply with me, intending on starting the double dose after I drove home.

I slipped the phone into my purse, took two ibuprofen, and began preparing for the dinner with Stephen Andersen. After setting the dining table with an aqua cloth and white candles, I made a salad, prepped the swordfish with lemon juice and fresh herbs from the garden, and hurried into the master bedroom on the opposite wing of the house. Peeling off my clothes, I walked into the bathroom, which adjoined the guest room. The porcelain tub was old and deep, with stubby feet, and was encircled by an ill-fitting canvas curtain. The metal drain was stained with rust, and a long weeping orange line edged in lime green extended below the faucet.

I turned on the water, stepped under the cool spray, and felt the day's heat and the ocean's salt disappear as I shampooed and rinsed my hair. Then, placing my feet on the bathmat, I cautiously extricated myself from the tub and sat on a low stool. With a large towel, I dried my body, staring at it with critical eyes—the loss of muscle tone and firmness, the pallor that showed where my skin hadn't been exposed to sunlight. Sixteen pounds had been shed because of the days I couldn't eat or couldn't eat much. While I had always been slender, if I continued at this rate, I would soon be in trouble. The oncologist warned me to maintain my weight. She did not need to explain why.

I brushed my shoulder-length hair and checked that there weren't too many strands caught in the brush, an anxiety that I couldn't quell. All was fine. After returning to the bedroom, I rummaged through my newly purchased two-sizes-smaller clothes and chose white cotton slacks and a pale pink blouse embroidered with ivory flowers. White sandals, pearl earrings, and a gold bracelet completed my outfit. Sitting in front of the makeup mirror, I added eyeliner and lipstick. With the light color on my face, I almost looked healthy. Even my green eyes were bright, leading me to wonder whether an afternoon at the beach or Stephen Andersen was the cause of this small rejuvenation. If it was due to Stephen, then what was I anticipating? Because of my preoccupation with the divorce, I hadn't given much thought to our evening except to recall how magnificent he looked rushing out of the ocean and to wonder why a handsome younger man would opt for a quiet meal in Truro when he could participate in the scintillating nightlife offered in Provincetown. Of course, he might leave after dinner and visit the clubs, whose clientele arrived late.

I moved to the bed and sat on the blue and green chenille spread. What did I want? Company? A few hours of pleasant conversation? Only on rare occasions had I asked a man for dinner—my publisher and two male colleagues. Tonight didn't fall into the collegial category, though I wasn't sure how to typify it. Not a date, certainly. No, just a friendly get-together.

"He's a gay guy, Bess," I said, gathering my hair in a barrette. "Just have a good time."

I often held these little tête-ê-têtes with myself, as if from assured therapist to confused client. And then I would laugh, as I did now.

———

At six, Stephen's white sedan cautiously navigated the ruts and twists of the driveway. I watched as he parked next to my car, stepped out with two brown bags in his arms, and began walking up the gray slate path, looking like a glowing vision, with his neatly combed white hair and his pale complexion only faintly colored from the outing on the beach. It seemed that the evening sun was magically attracted to him, striking his blue eyes, his white Oxford shirt, whose sleeves were rolled to the elbows, and his Bermuda-length white poplin shorts. Beside his iridescent figure, the dunes and foliage diminished, as if outshone and outclassed.

"Hello!" I held the door open for him, thinking he looked very preppy with his navy boat shoes and red canvas belt.

Stephen grinned and gave me a quick kiss on the cheek. He was wearing a summery cologne that reminded me of cool, blue water. "Greetings! I came prepared," he said, pointing his chin toward the two grocery bags.

He entered the living room and headed for the kitchen without asking where it was. Inside, Stephen tipped his head to avoid the low ceiling, though he cleared the rafters by nine inches, and set the bags on the counter. From the smaller one, he removed a box of Godiva chocolates.

"It was candy or flowers. Not too imaginative, I'm afraid."

I thanked him and confessed to having a weakness for chocolate. "I forgot dessert, so this will be it. Thank you."

Stephen reached into the other bag and set bottles of Muscadet, Sancerre, and an Alsatian pinot blanc on the counter. "Couldn't decide."

"I love all three. Shall we start with the pinot blanc?"

—

Once our glasses were filled, I brought Stephen down a short hall to the studio because I thought he might be interested in the owners' artwork.

"Both the husband and wife are artists," I told him, opening the door. "I haven't met them—we've only spoken on the phone when I arranged the rental."

The room smelled of turpentine and oil paints and was crowded with a tall brown easel, a glass-topped folding palette, numerous canvases and sketchbooks stored in vertical racks, paintings hung crooked on the walls, bookcases jammed with art books and still-life props, and grimy, paint-smeared marmalade jars stuffed with brushes. I liked the chaos and I liked the paintings; most were realistic land and seascapes, but there were some interior studies and a few portraits.

Stephen admired the work, explaining that his tastes ran to more graphic and abstract art. "That's because I can't draw like this." He pointed to a pencil sketch tacked to the wall. "I took a few art classes at Cornell, but I wasn't very talented."

Stephen stared at the supplies and the easel with a trace of wistfulness, or so I thought.

"I'm sure that's not true."

He shrugged, as if in deference to my opinion. "Well, okay, you're right, I'm not absolutely terrible. I'd love to try painting again. Acrylics probably, because I lack the patience for oils."

"Then you should. What's preventing you, Stephen?" This came out sounding like one of my professional comments.

He looked surprised and laughed. "Ah, good therapy, maybe?"

I felt my cheeks warm with embarrassment. "Yes, you're right. Sorry. But it's still a valid question."

"It is. I'll think about it. I don't have much leisure time these days," he added, "but then again I suppose that's the wrong attitude. I need to allot time on my schedule, like I do for my business activities."

"That doesn't sound very…well…spontaneous."

Stephen chuckled. "Spontaneous?" He examined me more closely, like a subject and not as a person, his eyes running over my face, perhaps analyzing its angles, colors, and textures. "Hey, okay. Let's be spontaneous. Why not?" He hefted a Windsor chair and placed it by the west-facing window, under a skylight. "Bess, would you please move over here?"

When I hesitated, Stephen laid his hands on my shoulders and steered me to the chair. I sat and he adjusted my position so the sun fell onto my face. Using his fingertips, he perfected the tilt of my head before announcing that the pose was perfect.

I laughed, feeling embarrassed, and watched Stephen cross the room and remove one of the smaller sketchbooks from the racks as well as two pencils and a kneaded eraser from a wooden taboret.

"Do you think anyone would mind if I used a sheet of paper?" he asked.

"No, probably not."

"Good."

Stephen rolled a metal stool to a spot about two yards away, propped his feet on the lowest rung, and began drawing with sure and practiced strokes. Although I couldn't see the page, I assumed he was establishing the dominant shapes first; next, he began smudging lines with his finger to create tone, occasionally lightening areas with the eraser. He kept one pencil clenched between his lips, mostly using a common 2B pencil, but occasionally alternating to one with a darker lead.

I remained silent, though I felt ill at ease. In sessions, clients observed me but were so involved in their own thoughts and feelings, working through what they planned to say next, that I was almost invisible. In fact, it's my belief that people don't really see each other acutely except for very rare moments of heightened emotion, yet they unconsciously absorb details of behavior and expression that their brains sort into a series of generalized images. Therefore, while I was accustomed to casual observation, Stephen's intense scrutiny was unusual in my experience. What did I look like to him and what had inspired him to reach for the pencil to record my image? Was it a fascinating play of light, a fleeting mood on my face, or had I misjudged the nature of his interest entirely?

I sat there as calmly as I could, musing over whether Stephen was gay, bisexual, or straight; whether his eyes revealed any sexual attraction. I didn't think so, but Stephen was a cipher.

After about twenty minutes, he stopped and took a sip of wine. I did the same.

"Well, I didn't expect to do that!" Stephen said, smiling.

"May I see?"

He squinted at his handiwork, sighed as if unsure of its merit, and finally offered the sketchbook. "It's not very good, I'm afraid."

The drawing featured part of the wall and window in the background, with my head and upper body rendered in a mixture of tight detail and simple, impressionistic lines. What surprised me the most was that Stephen had created a younger version of myself, a portrait of a woman in her early forties who no longer existed. How had he accomplished this when he had never met me then? My light brown hair, gathered with a barrette—as it was in reality—appeared thicker than it actually was and almost sensual, swooping down from my temples and partially covering my ears; my eyes gazed out from the page with steadiness, lit from the side and top by the sun, which produced a luminous effect despite the limitations of the pencil medium. My newly etched wrinkles, engraved by illness, were missing as was the slight droop of my eyelids that had become more pronounced because of weariness and pain. Overall, Stephen had caught my expression well: the mild amusement exemplified by a small upturn of my lips, the gaze that conveyed openness, yet he had also managed to imply an inner reserve, though I couldn't explain how this subtle complexity could be captured in such a quick study. It seemed that Stephen possessed strangely accurate knowledge about me.

"The likeness is excellent, Stephen!"

"Thank you."

"But I think you've done me a service…making me appear so—"

"Beautiful?" he asked.

I glanced at the sketchbook, disconcerted. It had been decades since anyone had described me as beautiful. I didn't think of myself that way, not then and especially not now. "It's a very flattering portrait."

"I don't consider it flattering."

"Well, it is. And I'm twenty years younger. How did you know—"

"What you looked like then?" Stephen chuckled. "Oh, you wouldn't want me to reveal secrets of the trade."

This inscrutable remark felt odd. "So, can you age me as well?" I said this in a teasing manner.

He studied me closely, much as he had a few minutes ago. "No, Bess. Sorry. I can't do that."

I started to ask why not and didn't. His answer came across as ambiguous, although underscored with significance. Perhaps he couldn't envision me as an older woman because I would never live to be one? If this were true, how did he know that? From noticing the port in my chest or was my encroaching death written on my face?

"It's a lovely drawing, Stephen."

He gave me a modest smile. "I'm glad you like it, but I can do better. Maybe one of these days I'll paint a real portrait."

"Of me?"

"Why not?"

I could think of some obvious reasons, such as that Stephen lived in Boston and I lived hours away in southwestern Connecticut, that we were only acquaintances who would spend an evening together and then return to our separate lives. Even so, something about his suggestion, put forth with a touch of humor, carried weight and intention. Stephen seemed serious about continuing our relationship into the future, past our days here, as if this was already settled between us. This did not disturb me at all—far from it—but I couldn't shake the feeling that he had known me prior to our meeting this afternoon, thus being able to visualize my younger appearance. Yet, if I had ever encountered Stephen before, I wouldn't have forgotten him.

I returned the sketch to Stephen, who carefully tore it out of the spiral-bound pad.

"A keepsake," he said.

I accepted the page, came to my feet, and was instantly assailed by a bout of vertigo. While this was not an unusual occurrence of late, I wondered if the sensation was due to sickness, the heady fumes of turpentine, or whether the drawing had caused my momentary disorientation. I kept my hand on the back of the chair in order to disguise my unsteadiness, but Stephen was returning the pencils and sketchbook to their respective places and hadn't noticed.

I smiled at him and led the way down the hall.

4

We returned to the living room with a plate of cheese and crackers, the bottle of wine in a cooler, and our filled glasses. I sat in one of the armchairs, and Stephen took the sofa. There was a moment of awkward silence, which I broke.

"So, Stephen, forgive my curiosity, but why are you in Provincetown alone? Assuming you are alone—I recall you said that you knew no one here."

He took a sip of his drink. "Yeah, I'm by myself. Like you are?"

"Yes."

"Well, I suppose the sea called to me," he said, with a smile. "Mostly, I didn't want to stay where I was."

"I can understand that."

He looked at me to see if I was merely agreeing with him or admitting to a similar feeling and then continued. "As may be the case with you, Bess, I think more clearly by the ocean. Though there is plenty of water near Boston, this area is more conducive. Quieter...except for the town itself."

"I agree," I replied. "How long have you been here?"

"I came a few days ago. Haven't decided when I'll leave." He stared inside his wine glass, as if it held the answer.

"Are you on vacation?"

"Sort of."

His enigmatic response made me unsure whether to pursue this topic of conversation. I sensed Stephen was hesitant to talk more about it.

"You mentioned earlier that you're an insurance broker. Are you still working?" I asked, wondering if his business was failing and that was the cause for his departure.

"Yes, I am, but since I freelance, I have control over my schedule. Plus my clients are all over the country, reachable by phone and email. I can set up shop almost anywhere."

"Is it possible to make a decent living doing this? Without working in an office with a permanent address?"

"Sure. I do fairly well. It seems I have a knack for selling policies to the right people."

"The right people?"

"Yeah, those who will live a long time and pay premiums for years."

"As compared to those who won't live long and buy a policy shortly before their death?"

"Yes, pretty much."

"How do you know who is healthy and who isn't? Do your clients need physical examinations? I confess that I know very little about this type of insurance."

"No. There are some application questions, but I rely mostly on instinct." Stephen shrugged. "I don't know. I just seem to have dumb luck or crazy intuition. I went into business soon after college."

"Really? How old are you, Stephen?"

He chuckled. "I'm timeless."

I laughed at this and thought his assessment was accurate. Stephen wasn't old and wasn't young, just perfect. "And you don't even wear a watch!"

This made Stephen laugh again. "Very clever! No watch, no time." He shook his head at my joke. "And you, Bess? What about your therapy practice?"

"I've recently closed it, though I hold occasional phone sessions."

"Got burned out?"

"A little but that's not why. I'll explain in a minute. Let me start the rice first."

I walked into the kitchen, feeling reluctant to relate my medical situation, whose repetition became more rote each time, like I was describing someone else's tragedy. But there was no way to dodge the issue. After adding the rice to the boiling water, I returned to my chair.

"You were saying?" Stephen prompted.

"Oh, yes. Talking about my decision to stop working…well, it's complicated."

"Because of why you're doing it?" Stephen observed me with his pale blue eyes. In the sun, they had glittered with gem-like intensity; now, inside, they were darker and more opaque.

"Yes," I said, drinking some wine. "I've ended my career because I have Stage IV pancreatic cancer." I hesitated, to allow this information to settle. "I've been undergoing numerous chemo treatments, but I was given a little break this summer. Probably they will begin again shortly, so this might be my last opportunity to get away."

"Oh, Bess! I'm sorry!" He said this with unfeigned regret and without the dripping sympathy that makes me so uncomfortable. "When were you diagnosed?"

"Thirty months ago."

He looked surprised, probably because very few pancreatic cancer patients live so long.

"I was feeling queasy for a few weeks and went to see my internist, who sent me to a gastroenterologist. After an MRI and a biopsy, she diagnosed Stage IV."

"No real warning, then?"

"No. That's why this kind of cancer kills so quickly. It's very aggressive. When people first suspect they might be sick, it's more or less too late." I shifted slightly in my chair to ease the pressure against my back. "I've already outlived my prognosis. By quite a lot."

Sometimes I look away after this confession because I don't want to intrude on a person's private reaction, nor am I happy about exporting my sorrow onto someone else. While I know many terminal patients become addicted to telling everyone about their illnesses, as if in doing so they can dilute their feelings or even magically erase the disease itself, I'm not one of them. In fact, I'm embarrassed to speak about my cancer. With Stephen, I felt differently. My eyes remained on his as he moved to the edge of the sofa and grasped my hand.

"I'm sure you have an excellent oncologist?"

"Yes. Dr. Melbourne in Stamford and a specialist in New York, who I see a few times a year."

"Do you get on well with Dr. Melbourne?"

"I suppose so. I have no idea how she feels about me, but she's probably exhausted answering all of my questions. At each appointment, I quiz her about the latest bloodwork results, though that seems about as helpful as reading tea leaves. In response, she usually replies, 'Well, yes, it could mean that or it could mean…'" I shook my head. "I suspect oncologists possess low-affect personalities and are cozy with ambiguity, especially when dealing with Stage IV cancer."

"And the doctor in New York?"

"She sounds more definitive, though she incorrectly predicted my longevity. Frankly, a five-dollar psychic wearing gigantic hoop earrings and swathed in a colorful turban might be as insightful." I paused. I was being too glib about a serious subject. "The bottom line, Stephen, is that no one knows when I will vacate my place on earth, but I'm now much closer to sooner rather than later."

He looked sad. "That must be the hardest part. Not knowing."

"It is." I gave him a small smile. "I'm sorry to go on about this. To be honest, I don't like talking about the subject. It may sound crazy, but having the disease seems like a personal failure of some kind, although mine is due to a BRCA2 gene mutation inherited from my father. He died from stomach cancer."

"So you did nothing to cause what happened," Stephen replied. "But knowing that doesn't really help, does it?"

"No, it doesn't. Here I am…a professional who deals with

irrational thoughts in others, and I can't eradicate my own irrational thinking."

Stephen pressed my hand and let it go. "You're too tough on yourself." He said this in a near whisper, then gazed out the windows, thinking. "I appreciate the dichotomy in your admission, Bess. That although you understand the cause is genetic, you still feel like the cancer is somehow your fault."

"That I deserved to get it…for some reason."

"Yes," he said, facing me again. "I think there are two types of people—those that take no responsibility for why they are sick, who want to take a pill or find a surgeon to 'fix' a bad back, for example, rather than altering their posture and the habits that caused the problem. And those like yourself who take too much responsibility."

"In either case, no one deserves to die prematurely, regardless of the cause. I've dealt with several end-stage patients and know how frightening the experience is. Now, of course, it's personal."

Stephen turned philosophical. "Life is fragile. Most of us don't realize this until we encounter a terrible illness or have a serious accident."

"That's true," I agreed, thinking that Stephen was an unusually sensitive soul. "And to return to the idea of self-inflicted disease… many therapists believe—or used to believe—that cancer affects those who hold things in, especially anger and hurt. Creating a kind of hot festering inside. While there might be some element of truth in this—and how stressful periods in one's life seem connected to the onset growth of tumors—this correlation is generally being debunked by genetic research. Much in the way many mental illnesses are now attributed to brain abnormalities or inherited traits rather than traumas suffered in a toxic early environment, though it's my belief that physical science doesn't explain all psychological issues. Maybe not even most."

Stephen poured himself more wine and nodded. "And how does this apply to you?"

I chuckled at this. "I'm a professional absorber of pain and anger. That's my job—or was. And I tend to contain how I feel rather than expressing my emotions. Although this is an inherent tendency, I probably have become worse over the years."

"Because of your work…"

"Yes, and because of necessity." I realized I was opening the door to a discussion of my marriage and wasn't comfortable doing that. "Now, enough theorizing. Time to do some cooking."

—

After sliding the swordfish into the broiler, I turned toward Stephen. "You know, you're a very skilled listener and very sympathetic. You should have been a psychologist."

He laughed. "Oh, not me! I'm more of a doer than an advisor."

"Perhaps I should have advised less and done more." I smiled at him. "Anyway, I want to thank you for your response. Many people's comments aren't very welcome."

"How so?" He leaned against the kitchen countertop.

"Well, I have no idea about your religious beliefs, so forgive me if I'm being insensitive, but what really drives me crazy is when people say they'll pray for me. Whenever I hear this inane platitude, my stomach turns. For a while, I let these remarks pass until I couldn't tolerate the hypocrisy any longer and I began replying, 'Who are you praying to?' If they said, 'God,' I would respond, 'If there is a God—and there isn't—why should I pray to the entity that gave me cancer in the first place?' I'm afraid my perspective isn't always appreciated, but I've grown weary of monitoring everything I say."

"People usually tread lightly on the subject of religion. A holdover from days when there were fewer agnostics and atheists, and everyone accepted that a believer's point of view was the norm." Stephen laughed. "And, yes, Bess, probably no one expects you to be outspoken."

"I've always tried to be considerate of others," I replied. "Anyway, religion is a difficult issue. My husband, Hugh, a philosopher, can go on for hours about the subject. In my opinion,

God is merely a human construct designed to maintain power over people, a vestige from our primal superstitions."

"Something to hold onto when times get difficult?" A trace of a smile appeared. "Such as when a person is ill?"

I nodded, appreciating his subtle wit, and continued. "Death, dying, and fear create a craving for certainty, for someone all-knowing to be in charge, who understands the reason behind a tragic occurrence when we don't. Someone who can pull a miracle from his supernatural back pocket. It's not surprising that surgeons are compared to gods. We need them to be like that because it absolves us from taking responsibility for our decisions." I hesitated and then added, "I believe there's often no logic behind disasters— they just happen. And there's no supreme being orchestrating our daily lives."

"No giant puppet master?" He chuckled. "I tend to agree with you, Bess. However, I do believe each of us has a time."

I gave him a quizzical look.

"Yeah." Stephen didn't explain what he meant. Instead, he opened the refrigerator and withdrew the bottle of Sancerre. Before I could apologize in case I'd offended him, he reached for the corkscrew and began opening the wine, apparently unfazed by our conversation. As he poured wine into my glass, I almost stopped him because an oxycodone might be needed later. But tonight was special, and I gave myself permission to indulge.

—

When dinner was ready, we carried our plates to the table. I lit the white candles, and we sat perpendicular to each other. He tasted the fish, rice, and salad, complimenting each, and I relaxed, now that the stress of preparation was over and the hurdle of my cancer disclosure had been overcome.

As we had earlier, we shared anecdotes. Stephen demonstrated a wry sense of humor as he described the foibles of his clients.

"Yeah, one old guy was amazing. Turned out he was eighty-eight, with a pacemaker, multiple stents, one semi-functioning kidney, and severe emphysema. He insisted he was sixty-two and the picture of health despite having a chronic cough and phlegmy wheeze, which kept interrupting our phone conversation. When I informed him about the penalties for misrepresenting his medical condition, the man went dead silent—in fact, I thought he'd died on the spot. I kept saying, 'Mister McKenzie, Mister McKenzie, are you there?' Eventually, he fessed up to his true age and what ailed him. 'I guess I'm not a good candidate for life insurance, am I?' he asked. 'No, I don't think so,' I said."

"Poor guy!"

"I know. I felt sorry for him," Stephen admitted. "So, Bess, you must have some fascinating tales to tell."

"Yes, I do." Though I seldom discussed my clients, I matched Stephen story for story, not providing names. Dinner passed quickly as did the wine, so that when we had finished eating, scraped the dishes, and returned to the couch carrying the lit candles from the table, the bottle of Muscadet accompanied us. I could feel the effects of the alcohol and accepted only half a glass. Stephen took his previous seat and patted the place beside him, which again caused me to wonder where the evening was headed. I slipped off my sandals and tucked my feet under me, while he stretched his long legs under the coffee table.

"Forgive my curiosity," he said, laying his arm on the back of the sofa, "but I notice you're wearing a wedding ring. And you mentioned a husband?"

I glanced at my hand, at the gold band. When would I remove this symbol of marriage, one Hugh had never worn, most likely because he preferred not to telegraph his status to potential lovers? I twirled the ring and realized I already felt separated from Hugh.

"I'm married and have been for a long time. Not very happily." I paused to swallow some wine. "But soon, I won't be married at all."

"What? Is your husband walking out on you?" His voice tightened with outrage. "When you're sick?"

"No, that's not the case. The opposite, in fact. This afternoon I called my attorney to begin the process of divorce."

Stephen's eyes widened. "That's sort of surprising, isn't it? Ending a relationship when relationships are so important?" He offered this without criticism, as an observation. "Why now?"

"Why now? It's time to fix the one area in which I've haven't stood up for my principles. I've been fairly successful maintaining them in my professional capacity, but I should have set stricter boundaries with Hugh many years ago and enforced them when he wandered outside of our marriage."

"Giving him an ultimatum?"

"Yes." I sighed. "And the other reason is that I don't want to be a burden to anyone. I've never been before. I've always worked, taken care of my clients, my son, my husband, and, later in her life, my mother. No one has had to worry about me. Hugh especially."

"Isn't this an exceptional circumstance?"

I thought for a moment. "It is, but," I exhaled slowly, "to tell the truth, requiring support feels strange."

"Being in the role of one needing help instead of giving it?"

"Yes. Most of my life has been dedicated to providing outgoing assistance rather than the other way around."

Stephen considered this, nodding slightly, as if he agreed with me or shared a comparable experience. "I can sympathize with that."

"Because you're similar?"

"Mmm, a little," he replied. "But if your husband has been a disappointment—and it sounds like he has been—why not let him have a chance to make it up to you? I'd think that he would, if he cares."

"That's a reasonable hope in most instances…and, yes, I believe Hugh loves me in his own way. I suppose this is more my problem. I don't want to provide an easy out for him, one he doesn't deserve after decades of hurtful betrayal. That may be mean-spirited, but with our friends, he shapes the situation so that he looks like the heroic caretaker, a man who others should admire for his selfless devotion. Honestly? His behavior really infuriates me." I sighed again, trying to stanch the indignant feelings that were rising up.

"You don't believe he could support you for…"

Stephen was obviously reluctant to fill in the timeline blanks, nor had I mentioned the revised prognosis because there wasn't one. Most people knew how lethal pancreatic cancer was and tiptoed around the subject of longevity.

"I have no idea how many months I have, Stephen. But from the very beginning, Hugh has used my illness as a platform to grandstand, to focus attention on himself whenever we're socializing…even sometimes with my oncologist, on the occasions when he's come to an appointment with me. While I don't begrudge his sadness and grief, I don't want to begrudge my feelings, either. Again, this might seem petty and revengeful, but being consistently supportive is difficult for Hugh."

Stephen drank some wine and lowered his head for a moment, then searched my eyes. "I assume you've tried to talk to your husband."

"Yes, I have—often—but I can't change his nature. Perhaps when Hugh receives the divorce notification, he'll reflect on what he's done—the betrayals especially—but I'm not convinced he'll take responsibility for his numerous affairs or the way he's been acting recently."

"So you're worried he wouldn't be there for you?"

I rubbed my neck, hesitating to admit the truth. "I am. The thought that I would be really sick and he would fail me, well, I'd prefer paying an aide when friends aren't available rather than rely on Hugh." I shrugged, realizing I should stop, but before I could edit myself, I added, "I'm not entirely blameless. Perhaps I stayed with him because it allowed me to appear virtuous in contrast to Hugh. I have to consider this possibility…that part of me enjoys being in a superior moral role. Rather like being a psychotherapist who models proper thoughts and actions to others."

He remained grave despite my self-critical irony. "I doubt that's true."

I shook my head. "Well, I hope it isn't, but the idea nags at me from time to time. My friend Susan laughed at me when I mentioned this possibility."

"As well she should."

I sat for a moment and then apologized. "Stephen, I'm sorry if this diatribe against Hugh comes across as cold and angry, but that's the way I feel. I'm no longer emotionally close to my husband, and I'm upset with myself for letting Hugh treat me so badly. I should have divorced him years ago." I placed my hands on my face and felt the heat on my cheeks. "Oh, dear! I never spout off like this! Forgive me for blurting everything I've been worrying about."

Stephen smiled. "That's okay. I imagine all of this has been brewing for a long while. Good that you can talk about it."

"Even so, I'm sorry to hit you with all of these problems."

"Don't be."

He settled against the sofa and calmly folded his hands in his lap. His gaze remained steady, his face composed, without any hint of discomfort. Some people, whose lives were impoverished, existed in symbiotic relationship to others, finding nourishment in other people's illnesses, marital disasters, deaths, and tragedies large and small. Stephen clearly wasn't that type.

"I'm a bit of a mess, I'm afraid," I told him, trying to lighten my tone. "But at least I've made a decision about Hugh, which is good. Sometimes movement of any kind is a relief. That's what I tell my clients anyway."

"Being stuck isn't much fun," he replied. "Especially during a difficult point in one's life."

I followed my instincts. "Is that where you are?"

"Yeah. Sort of. I'm not so much stuck as unsure what to do next...waiting for that chance meeting. For someone to come along and take me down a new road or open a curtain on a new opportunity." He turned this idea over. "Maybe that qualifies as stuck, but I find that I'm often waiting." Stephen gave a short bark of laughter. "That sounds kind of passive. I should sally forth bravely into the world!"

"Can you say more about that?"

He laughed again. "Oh, my, the old therapist's line!"

"Sorry." It was my turn to smile. "Habit. A bad one."

Stephen poured wine into our glasses, more in his at my instruction. "Hey, I almost forgot! We need dessert!" He rose and went into the kitchen and retrieved the box of chocolates. Returning, he removed the plastic wrapper from the box, lifted its top, and offered the candy to me. I chose one filled with dark fudge. "Not sure Muscadet and chocolates are a marriage made in heaven," he said.

Stephen pressed me to take another, which I did, and then he ate two pieces of chocolate and settled on the couch, observing me as if weighing whether to make a confession.

"Okay, Bess, you wanted to know why I came to Provincetown."

"I do, yes."

"Well, I'm here because Provincetown is where Terry and I spent many special weekends."

5

~~~~~~

"Terry?"

His chin dropped onto his chest. "My boyfriend. My husband since April."

I was about to congratulate him, then noticed his sad expression. "Since April? Have you been together long before that?"

"A year. But this summer marked the beginning of, well, of magical thinking."

For a moment, I didn't follow where Stephen was going. "As in Joan Didion's book?" He nodded. "It dealt with her reactions to her husband's death."

"Yes, it did." Stephen didn't elaborate, just sat quietly, chewing on his lip. Finally, he said, "Magical thinking: the what-if questions. What if I had done this or that, and we could have avoided the outcome. Or if I returned to Provincetown now, could I redo everything that happened? Start over." His mouth gathered at one side, as if he was disgusted by these nonsensical wishes.

"Which is why you're on the Cape?"

"Yes. We held our wedding here." Stephen moved so he could face me directly. "I proposed to Terry in March. I wanted to show how much I cared, how I would be there for him until the end. To make the ultimate commitment." He hesitated before adding, "I suppose it's ironic, Bess. You're ending your marriage because you're sick, and I married Terry because he was sick. Not that I wouldn't have done so at some point. We were talking about it before his diagnosis."

I let another silence float between us, hoping Stephen would continue. However, he seemed mired in his own thoughts. "What was wrong with Terry?"

"Well, absolutely nothing at first. We were introduced at a pool party on Fire Island, a place where I've spent a lot of time. Terry was incredibly fit, a fine athlete, full of energy. We talked and immediately liked each other, so I asked him to play tennis the next afternoon." Stephen gave a dry laugh. "He beat me. Two sets to one. And bought me a beer afterward. That's how we started." He reached for his glass and took a swallow of wine. "Everything was going great. I moved to Boston, to Terry's condo, and settled in. I thought my search for the right guy was over. There was no friction. No arguments or drama or misunderstandings. I was really happy. Then Terry began having these strange night sweats, his appetite disappeared, he lost weight and became tired for no reason. When he developed pain in his left side, we knew something was seriously wrong. We went to Mass General, and, after a lot of tests, they diagnosed him with T-Cell-Prolymphocytic Leukemia—or T-PLL—and an enlarged spleen. Terry was given chemo but kept developing infections that impeded treatment. We did rounds of antibiotics and began again."

"Oh, Stephen! How terrible!"

"It was. A complete nightmare." He set down his glass, closed his eyes, and pinched the bridge of his nose. When he removed his fingers and looked at me again, tears had formed. "Last spring, he seemed a little better so we decided to get married in Provincetown because we'd spent many special weekends here. Although it was the end of April, it was a very windy day on the beach. Terry wore a hat and a coat and still was cold. Probably it was stupid to subject him to the weather, but this was where he wanted to hold the service."

"Was this on the beach where you and I met?" I asked.

Stephen nodded. "Yes, it was. An odd coincidence perhaps.

When I saw the port on your chest," he said, "I knew you were also ill. Terry had one inserted too."

"Is that why you kept talking to me?"

He smiled. "That and you saved my life."

"Let's not go that far!" I took a small sip of wine and became serious again. "And after the wedding?"

"After that?" Stephen stared into the dim room, remembering. "Well, we spent the week struggling to have a normal honeymoon. We went out for dinner, which he could hardly eat, and tried to dance at a disco, but he couldn't do that, either. Terry was fading fast. His lymph nodes became more swollen as did his spleen. He started coughing. The pain medication wasn't working. It was clear that we had entered a new stage, the beginning of a steep descent." He turned to observe me closely. "You may not be familiar with this type of leukemia, but the average survival is about eight months. Of course, we both thought Terry would live a lot longer because he had been in excellent health. In fact, we kept talking like he would beat the disease altogether."

The weight of his sorrow fell heavily upon me, and I struggled against the desire to sink back against the sofa. "I can appreciate why you were so optimistic, considering Terry's age and physical fitness. That just added to the surreal nature of the situation," I replied. "Yet, sad as it was, this time together in Provincetown must have been precious to you. And certainly meant a great deal to Terry."

"It did. But it was like this guillotine was hanging over our heads, ready to fall without warning. We were acutely aware of every moment, both those that were happy and those that caused us to worry. By the fourth day, we knew Terry belonged in the hospital."

I felt my chest tighten. I too sensed a guillotine about to fall and had privately used that same metaphor over the last months. I thought of Hugh and wondered if he shared that reaction, if he feared the sudden loosening of the lethal blade. The fact that I wasn't sure if Hugh was fearful was a significant indication that our marriage, our relationship, was a failure at a time when we should have come together for comfort.

"I'm so sorry, Stephen." I said this with deep sincerity. It took no imagination to appreciate how the honeymoon had transformed from a time of beauty into a time saturated with grief and anxiety. "I'm sure you were devastated. And Terry? Your love and vow of marriage must have been a solace to him…to know you would be at his side until the end, though he probably tried his best to hide how sick he felt, to allow the two of you to recreate those special early weekends."

"He did but it was obvious that he was dying. Terry had the most beautiful brown eyes, yet they no longer seemed to have any color."

Stephen's focus intensified, causing me to wonder if my green eyes had also lost color. I thought of the monochromatic portrait and wished it had been rendered in paint so I could see the woman Stephen had envisioned, the woman I'd once been.

Several tears slid down his cheek. He brushed them away and continued. "Terry looked lost, defeated. When I suggested we return to Boston, he argued with me about it, probably trying to forestall what lay ahead. More magical thinking, perhaps. If we could hide out in our hotel room, death couldn't find him." Stephen shook his head. "But death knew exactly where he was. When Terry developed a fever, we had to leave. I bundled him in a blanket and carried him to the car. He slept most of the way, waking only when the pain spiked." Stephen shook his head. "I felt so useless."

I reached for his hand and held it. It felt large and cool in mine. "There was nothing you could do, Stephen. Against this disease you had no power. I understand how frustrated and scared you were."

Stephen chased another tear with his fingers and nodded. "I didn't even bother to drive us to the condo. Terry was admitted at Mass General and given IV antibiotics because an infection had set in, which the doctors said was pneumonia. Although he'd been scheduled for a stem-cell transplant the following week, this never happened. Terry started hospice and transferred home in the program. He died in my arms, thirteen days later, on a Tuesday morning."

"Oh, Stephen…" I squeezed his hand gently.

He bowed his head. "I'm sorry, Bess," he whispered. "I shouldn't impose on you, not now when you're dealing with so much. It's just that I feel so cut off from everyone. Being a couple and then becoming single again…it's like my identity was erased when I lost Terry. Even our friends were Terry's because he was from Boston. And most of them are married or in long-term relationships. They've been nice, but when I'm with them, it's awkward. Like I'm almost more alone than when I'm by myself."

"What about your family? Your close friends? Have they supported you?"

"I don't have relatives. And not many friends in the city." He sighed. "I've moved around a lot."

"I see." This additional example of Stephen's transience made me wonder afresh about his enigmatic life. He seemed like the type of man who should be surrounded by people and not just those who would be drawn to his physical attractiveness. Stephen was a very decent guy, with a thoughtful, friendly, and engaging personality. Yet, from his description, it sounded like Stephen had assimilated into Terry's life rather than integrating his own life with his partner's.

In a voice choked with misery, he said, "Oh, how I miss Terry! I thought I'd feel better by now, after all these months, but if anything I feel worse."

"Changes like you're going through, transitioning, can be extremely difficult, very confusing and disorienting."

We were silent while Stephen fought to regain his composure. At last, he said, "And even his friends—our friends—are acting weird."

"How do you mean?"

"Weird. Like…well…we were never married…like they don't

recognize my grief and how overwhelmed I am by Terry's death." He removed a tissue from his pocket and dried his cheeks.

"Why do you think that?"

"From comments some of them have made. One said I should go for a weekend in New York City—you know, visiting gay bars in the Village. Another tried to fix me up with a date. And, god! Terry's funeral had only been a month before! I couldn't believe it."

"People need at least a year to recover from the death of a spouse. Often a lot longer." I let my hands drop into my lap but remained leaning toward Stephen. "Maybe your friends were just trying to cheer you up, though I understand how that would make you feel alienated."

"I probably shouldn't be surprised." Stephen sighed. "This is going to sound narcissistic, but I've always been treated differently because I'm good-looking. I know I am—I can't deny it. But this one superficial attribute makes everyone think my feelings are superficial too. That someone like me can't feel deeply, that it will take no effort for me to replace Terry so his death shouldn't matter as it would to someone else."

I listened to his admission and couldn't recall hearing this remark before, that beauty was a source of negative prejudice. While it was sometimes assumed that pretty women couldn't also be intelligent—an irritating attitude—his experience seemed like a more comprehensive bias. I considered the most attractive people I had known—none as attractive as Stephen—and not one had ever expressed encountering similar discrimination.

"So, if I hear you correctly, Stephen, people deny that you can have profound feelings because you're handsome?"

"Yeah. Ever since I was young, I've been expected to be optimistic because nothing should go wrong for me. My life is supposed to be a happy cruise, like I've been granted a free pass, and like I should automatically excel at everything because of my appearance. Any successes—even those accomplished with maximum effort—are attributed to my looks. Not my talent or hard work. If I fail, then it's because I'm shallow or was tripped up by vanity and have no right to be upset." He shook his head. "And, no, my life hasn't always been easy."

"This sounds like an insidious form of jealousy. Of your good fortune, which—in people's minds—wasn't earned," I said, wondering about Stephen's past before Terry's death. "I assume Terry didn't feel that way, did he?"

"No, he understood. He loved me for myself. Oh, Bess, I'll never find anyone like him!" Stephen sat, shoulders hunched, downcast. "So how can I change the way everyone views me? Except to grow old or have some kind of horrible disfiguring accident."

"Obviously you can't. I'm sorry to hear your friends aren't respecting your loss. That's sad and makes me a little angry."

His desolate expression was wrenching. Whether it was the effect of the alcohol or the awareness of my own circumstances, which rose to the surface without much stimulus, I felt his grief keenly, with surprising force. In an odd way, his emotion blended into my own, though I normally was very good at maintaining a divide between myself and my clients. But Stephen wasn't a client, and we weren't sitting in my office for a session.

He moved closer. Suddenly, I became more aware of our proximity to one another. His modulated voice, placed in a low register, resonated faintly in the space between us. His breath was warm on my face, with a sweetness that overcame the scent of the wine, drawing me forward despite my reservations. Usually, with two heterosexuals, this moment might segue into a kiss, but Stephen was gay and could be turning to me because I was a therapist, in which case my response was clearly prescribed— allowing something more to develop, when he was in mourning, wasn't ethical. But I was in mourning, too, for the life I was about to lose. Did that cancel out my reservations? His cologne surrounded me, with a fragrance that seemed to translate into color. Like a dark turquoise ocean or a deep blue night sky.

"I don't know what I'm going to do, Bess."

While my fourth glass of wine remained on the coffee table

almost untouched, Stephen had drunk nearly two bottles of wine, which could easily contribute to an unstable mood, but the plaintiveness he expressed was sincere.

"Tonight there's nothing you can do," I replied. "And maybe not tomorrow, either. You're at the beginning of a long process of reestablishing yourself. I understand how steep the path ahead looks and know nothing I say will take away the sorrow. It exists and is a necessary part of the healing that will eventually occur. In some ways, the pain is beneficial, a warning not to go too fast. Kind of like with a broken leg. When there's too much discomfort, you know not to place weight on it. The important thing is to stay with your emotions rather than try to outrun or bury them. Whether your friends are supportive or not, this exploration is mostly your undertaking. A lonely one."

When I finished, to my surprise, he raised his hands and cupped my face. His touch was strangely intimate, very unlike Hugh's perfunctory caresses that had lost meaning for both of us. I caught my breath and gazed at Stephen. I had no idea what he was about to do, and no idea what I wanted him to do.

6

~~~~

The single moment seemed to stretch into minutes. I thought about my marriage, about Hugh, and the fact that I was no longer bound to him. While I had made one major decision this afternoon, it had never occurred to me that I would be faced with a romantic choice ever again. An eerie giddiness surged through these considerations, a *who-cares?* attitude. I attributed this reaction to the wine and my depleted condition, the dream-like presence of such a spectacular man. His mood had also greatly affected me, conjuring my own feelings of grief, loss, fear, and sadness. Although we were in different stages, on opposite sides of death, with Stephen reacting to what had happened and me reacting to what would happen, we shared a unique commonality. I placed my hands on his solid shoulders, intending on keeping him at arm's length, but the unhappiness in his eyes drew me in.

"Bess, you understand. You're so in tune with people…I bet you even put yourself in their shoes when you tell them about your illness. You sympathize with them rather than allow them to sympathize with you."

I hadn't thought about this, but perhaps Stephen was right. During each telling—and more frequently as the repetitions increased—I detached myself from being the subject, as if describing a third person who had cancer. A second cousin, perhaps, or an old college roommate. Probably protecting myself from being disappointed, a reaction that had slowly evolved from years of dealing with Hugh. And, yes, I did worry about the person I was confiding in. I always had. "I guess it's easier for me to do that. I've never liked being the center of attention. Now especially."

He covered my fingers with his and moved our hands into the space between us. "And I've never been comfortable in that position, either, though I can do little about it. There are times I'd like to fade into the wallpaper, but I can't. Everything I do is noticed. So, in a way, I know how you feel."

His pale blue eyes pulsed in the flickering candlelight. Was he trying to mesmerize me? Was this the beginning of a seduction? My head churned with conflicting impulses. I should retreat to my end of the sofa and reach for my wine glass in order to insert a separation between us. But I felt bewitched, swiftly and suddenly, by a magnetic attraction to Stephen, a physical yearning that was impossible to ignore. It had been forty years since I'd kissed another man besides my husband, a realization that hit me like a hand slap and also renewed my misgivings about Stephen's interest. Why would he be attracted to a woman and a woman my age?

"Stephen…" I began to say that we shouldn't act on our desires during such a highly charged emotional moment, but he brought his face nearer.

"Bess, we're alone in this house. Far from everyone we know. Your husband isn't here, and neither are my friends."

"Yes, we are." I heard the nervousness in my voice and wished I hadn't spoken.

Stephen's gaze didn't waver. "Bess, you know I want to kiss you."

I hesitated to respond, unsure what to do, and nodded.

He leaned over and touched my lips with his. The kiss was light and tentative, yet not at all brotherly. I reacted in kind, ready to stop, to laugh at our behavior, but Stephen placed his arms around me and really kissed me. Despite my therapist's morality, the frantic warnings shooting off in my mind, I kissed him with equal fervor. As if from a long slumber, my body awoke and caught fire, slowly at first, then with increased heat. Stephen's embrace was powerful yet his strength did not convey dominance, only care and tenderness. Excitement lofted me high on its momentum.

Stephen stood and helped me to my feet. As we pressed against each other, I felt his arousal. I began to speak, but he covered my mouth with his fingers and whispered, "Don't talk, Bess. Just feel."

He leaned down and extinguished all the candles except one. Grasping its candlestick, he placed his hand on my arm, and we left the living room, walking down the hall into my bedroom. When Stephen set the candle on the end table, I thought about condoms, which I didn't have, and safe sex, which should be practiced because Stephen was possibly a high-risk partner. On the other hand, after a hysterectomy, I couldn't get pregnant, and the concern about contracting a disease seemed faintly ridiculous given my medical future.

Stephen stood in front of me. "I've been tested, Bess. So don't worry about that."

I watched as he unbuttoned his white shirt and tossed it on a chair. His chest was as beautiful as I remembered: smooth, hairless, the muscles clearly defined. His skin was pale except for a light pink on his shoulders and arms.

"Okay," I replied, distracted by the vision before me.

Stephen kicked off his shoes, stepped forward, and raised my blouse over my head. Without hesitation, he reached to unhook my bra, which he did in one deft move, making me wonder how much experience he'd had with women. As my breasts were uncovered, I gasped slightly.

"You're very beautiful, Bess," he whispered.

I wanted to disagree; instead, I watched Stephen loosen his belt and scoop off his shorts and briefs. Then he unzipped my pants and brought them and my underwear to the floor. I trailed a line from his shoulders down to his biceps, noting the sinuous, muscular curves, and let my hands come to rest around Stephen's forearms. We stood in the wavering candlelight, savoring the moment, and came together.

—

When I awoke, it was early morning. My back hurt and I was sore all over—the port, my breasts, and from having intercourse several times, not to mention I was feeling exhausted. Although I was desperate for a painkiller, I didn't want to move from the bed, to wake Stephen, who was turned away from me, breathing quietly. I lay there, half within the pale blue sheets and half uncovered, and thought of what I'd done with a mixture of happiness and sadness. It had been more than a year since Hugh and I had made love, and it had been only an obligatory coupling. Although I had always blamed Hugh for the disintegration of our love life, I also shared some responsibility. Perhaps I had been too restrained, too cerebral for Hugh's taste, thus driving him into the arms of more highly sexed, demonstrative women.

I recalled his first lover, one of a lengthy list that stretched to the present. Chelsea had been a philosophy grad student and Hugh was her mentor—that's how he later represented their relationship. She had long blond hair and a curvaceous figure emphasized by wearing form-fitting blouses with plunging necklines—at least that was true on the occasion I saw her, on the afternoon when I visited one of Hugh's lectures to ask him to sign a check. When I arrived in the doorway above the hall, the class had already left, but Chelsea and Hugh were sitting in the second row of seats, his arm surrounding her. They were kissing, and he was helping himself to the contents of her peach-colored satin blouse.

Shocked, I fled the hall and rushed down the stairs to Susan Collier's office. Susan was a new best friend, a psychology professor, and a university counselor. She was ushering a student out the door after a session when I arrived. Seeing her kind face, my upset percolated into tears. She led me to her couch, whereupon I blurted out what I'd witnessed.

Susan placed a gentle hand on my shoulder. "Oh, Bess, I'm so sorry!"

The week before, she had cautioned me about Chelsea and

Hugh, having observed them in a suggestive clinch as she passed by Hugh's office. I told Susan she was mistaken, that I trusted my husband, yet I also trusted Susan. Doubt continued to gnaw at me for days until I encountered the scene in the lecture hall and Susan's warning had proved accurate.

I still remember how she looked at me, with her sympathetic gray eyes, as I said, "My god, Susan! We've been married only six months! What should I do?"

"I don't know. What do you feel like doing, other than bashing the bastard over the head?"

After all these years, her response—so typical of Susan—still made me smile. I remember grabbing a tissue from the box on the table and promising to talk with Hugh that night.

And I did. He insisted I hadn't seen anything, saying that Chelsea was crying about a recent break-up with a boyfriend, and he may have given her a quick, encouraging hug.

"But you were kissing her!"

He denied it.

And so it went, with his affairs and deceptions continuing, one after another. Eventually, I gave up accosting him because he lied about each woman, or, if caught outright, he apologized but didn't alter his actions. At least after the first affair, Hugh became more circumspect, though I still noticed the stray blond hair on his jacket, an errant whiff of perfume, and whenever a new girl came along, there were late nights. Living in such a suspicious state had corroded most of my romantic feelings for Hugh, even if I still harbored a tiny hope that he would change. He hadn't, though he often professed his love for me, and, in a way, he was being truthful, as, in a way, I was honest when I said I loved him. Discouraged, I retreated into my work, transferring personal passion into professional passion, donning the counselor's mask, a mask I sometimes didn't remove at home. No doubt this behavior wasn't conducive to sexual closeness, even if—from my perspective— Hugh's dalliances were the primary cause of our emotional and physical division. I thought about the electricity and desire I'd just felt with Stephen and realized I hadn't experienced this with my husband for many years. Why hadn't I found the courage to look elsewhere?

I considered how unguarded Stephen had been with me and how I'd responded in kind, meeting him with openness even if I felt shy about lying naked before his eyes. He had been a considerate lover, respectful of my fragility yet extremely adept and exciting. However, more than sexual release had happened, as pleasurable as that had been. What impressed me the most was the relief I experienced from our few hours of connection; the effect of being touched, of being reminded that I was still alive and able to give and receive affection. I hoped Stephen benefitted in a similar way, perhaps allowing him to forget about his sorrow for a short time, though I worried that he had thought of Terry during our lovemaking, which was probably unavoidable and very likely distressing for him. He hadn't said so, but in his situation, I would have been haunted by comparisons.

What would Stephen do next? Kiss me on the cheek, rush to his car, and drive off in a cloud of dust to his motel room or to Boston? Would I feel bereft and shattered if he did? I told myself once again that Stephen was gay, suffering from Terry's death, and had been under the influence of quite a lot of alcohol. Our union was probably one of those odd happenstances requiring the perfect alignment of place, time, and mood that wouldn't occur again. I shouldn't have any expectations, only take pleasure in the extraordinary night and be prepared to let Stephen go without any attempts to prolong the relationship.

But then he woke and turned toward me.

"Good morning, Bess." He smiled and slipped his arm under my head.

I moved closer, though as I did, the pain flared and spread like a hot spiderweb across the area below my shoulder blades. I shut my eyes, desperate to ignore the ache, and fervently wished I could concentrate on the warm feelings we shared and revel in the luxury of being protected by a strong, sensitive man. I even fantasized that maybe Stephen could magically ease my discomfort if I remained still. Yet the throbbing didn't stop.

I lay in his embrace, my head below his chin. Finally, I opened my eyes and pulled away. "Stephen, I'm sorry, but I need to take my medication."

His look of concern was affecting. "Are you all right?"

I shook my head. "No, not really. The pancreatic tumors press on my back. Sometimes it's not too bad, but lately, well..."

"I'm sorry, Bess. Can I get you something?"

"No, thanks."

Reluctantly, I separated from him and sat on the edge of the bed. As I was about to stand, my head began spinning. Afraid I might faint, I waited a few seconds, trying to focus on the cheerful, sunlit room and the positive mood created by Stephen. But neither the sunlight or Stephen could alleviate the pain or erase the dark, omnipresent awareness that the cancer was growing.

Feeling steadier, I rose and made my way around the bed, snatching my robe. In the bathroom, I poured a glass of water and shook out an oxycodone tablet from its orange container. After swallowing the pill, I frowned at the mirror, appalled at my face. Yesterday's color had faded, leaving a wan complexion; my expression was drawn; my eyes were pinched with pain. I tried not to think about my physical condition, how it was destroying the opportunity with Stephen, but I was angry. I thudded my palms against the sink and cursed the cancer.

Frustrated, I grabbed a wash cloth and scoured my face, then brushed my teeth and combed my hair. When I entered the bedroom, Stephen had slipped on his briefs and was waiting for me, his right arm stretched across my pillow.

"Are you any better?" he asked.

I climbed into bed beside him, trying to disguise how I felt. "Not yet. In another fifteen minutes. Once the oxycodone kicks in."

"And you're wearing a fentanyl patch, right?"

"Yes. My doctor said I could use two patches if I needed to."

Stephen encircled my shoulder. "Maybe you should. If it

controls the pain better."

The kindness in his voice made me want to dissolve into tears. "I might."

"I understand the worry about opioid addiction, but it doesn't really matter—"

"With terminal patients." I looked up at him. "I'm sorry, Stephen. The last thing I wanted was to ruin our morning together."

"It's okay."

"I'm sure you have things to do."

Stephen edged away a few inches so he could study me. "Bess, you haven't ruined anything. You can't help how you're feeling. Please don't give it another thought," he said. "And as for today, no, I don't have anything planned." He ran his fingers through my hair and smiled. "If you don't mind, I'd love to spend it with you."

I couldn't hide my surprise. "Really?"

Stephen laughed. "Yes, really. In fact, why don't I make breakfast while you stay in bed?"

His willingness to be with me was a relief as was having a few minutes for the painkiller to take affect. "Thank you."

He stroked my cheek. "Okay if I shower first?"

I explained where the guest towels were, and he disappeared into the bathroom.

—

Breakfast was grander than I would have made for myself. Fresh blueberries, scrambled eggs with cheese, toast with wild beach plum jelly, orange juice, and coffee. By the time Stephen placed the large brass tray on the bed, the pain had eased. He gave me a quick kiss, propped up the pillows, and sat to my right.

After a few minutes, I said, "I suppose we should talk about what happened."

Stephen cocked his head. "You first."

"I was rather hoping you would start," I replied, laughing.

"Hmm, let's see. You're going to ask me whether I'm gay, right?" He waited for me to nod in confirmation, which I did.

"Well, yes, I prefer men, although when I was in my twenties, I dated girls. I've never ruled out a relationship with a woman, so I suppose that makes me bisexual. In my opinion, I think that's normal or should be."

"I'm glad you've comfortable with yourself and aren't trying to fit into pre-set categories. I guess, in comparison, I've lived a conventional life. Whether this was a conscious choice or because I was too timid to experiment—I don't know."

"Or the right woman never came along."

"Maybe." I hesitated asking the question that loomed foremost in my thoughts: why had he chosen me? During my younger years, I might have understood his attraction, yet even then I had never dated a man who was as kind, thoughtful, and—though I hated to emphasize his looks—as handsome.

I swallowed some coffee and watched as he ate a corner of toast, his firm jaw moving with precision. In profile, his nose was straight, with only a modest flare at its end; his chin jutted outward, as did his brow, but neither feature lent an air of aggression. Instead, his face was open and unguarded, without pose or pretense or hint of guile or slyness. In fact, his personality appeared remarkably transparent, like still water rarely riled by negative impulses or feelings. How deep those waters were, I couldn't judge. It was quite possible that I was only seeing the surface and a little beyond, that his stunning beauty was blinding me to his neuroses, which we all had. While he had professed to be grief-stricken about Terry, what other issues was Stephen battling? He seemed confident—balanced and realistic in his appraisal of his strengths—yet his weaknesses weren't at all apparent. With a start, I realized I'd never felt the slightest friction with Stephen. Not one instance of disagreement or misunderstanding. It was all so smooth, like we were gliding together effortlessly. This was equally true of our lovemaking.

I ate the last of my blueberries and selected my words with care. "Stephen, this may not come out correctly, but I'm a little concerned that we shouldn't have slept together last night. It's so soon after Terry's death, and you're still mourning his loss." Although this was true, I was more disturbed that our intimate encounter hadn't been about me at all, that I had been a semi-blank canvas upon which he could paint Terry's image over mine.

He didn't answer. I hesitated and then added, "But that sounds like I'm pinning my anxieties on you. Instead, I should admit that I'm in a pretty fragile state these days. Fearful about endings rather than beginnings and trying to keep my life calm. Truthfully, I wasn't expecting anything to happen between us or to suddenly feel excited again."

"What's wrong with being excited, Bess?" He observed me carefully. "Or should I ask what are you afraid of?"

It was my turn to be quiet. I hadn't sorted through my thoughts and feelings, which I tended to mire in complexity. Stephen seemed to have a simple, straightforward approach, one I envied.

"I don't know. I'm afraid of a lot of things these days." I knew I was being vague and probably avoiding the truth. "Perhaps I fear rejection. We all do, but in my condition, it's hard for me to think anyone would chose to be with me. Especially someone who doesn't have to be involved."

"Someone like a stranger?"

I nodded. "Family and old friends are kind of stuck. You aren't."

"No, I'm not. Whatever I do is because I wish to do it." He reached over and stroked my arm. "And as for Terry and my grief and what we did last night, well, having sex with someone isn't always about having sex. Sometimes it's about comfort and kindness and feeling safe during tumultuous times…making a connection. We both need that right now." He twisted his lips into a wry smile. "Certainly we're swimming through high seas at the moment. Kind of appropriate that we met the way we did, wasn't it?"

"Yes, it was."

I realized I had placed myself in an almost post-physical realm after years of coping with Hugh's affairs. Even if my protective detachment had added to his disinterest, my husband was a man who loved the chase more than living with the capture. Being married had made me automatically less interesting. This caused me to wonder if Stephen would lose interest if I refused to have sex again or, for him, was sex only a conduit to closeness, as he had said?

I took a sip of coffee and laid down my cup. "It was a very special night."

"Oh?" He quickly swallowed some scrambled egg, wiped his mouth with a napkin, and stared at me with alarm. "Bess, that sounds like you're done with me. Have you changed your mind about us being together today?"

I was surprised by his reaction. "No, but I'd like to hear more about what you want, Stephen."

"Me?" His face relaxed and he flashed a suggestive look. "I don't think we're finished or at least I hope not."

While the evening with Stephen had been a high point in my sexual life, I was exhausted and sore and doubted that I could muster the strength to make love again. And yet, because so many of life's pleasures were rapidly dwindling, this might be one of my last chances to experience joy.

Stephen ate the last piece of toast, hoisted the tray off the bed, and carried it into the kitchen. Upon his return, he gave me a big grin, threw back the sheets, opened my robe, and began to seduce me with slow, tantalizing strokes.

7

~~~

Stephen's stamina and sensitivity were impressive, yet I couldn't shake the feeling that I'd plunged into an illusion of his creation, nor could I erase my doubts about why he was so attentive. Not that his lovemaking was mechanical or impassive—far from it— but I wasn't entirely sure he was excited by me.

When we came apart, I was perspiring. By comparison, Stephen hadn't broken a sweat, which was odd because he'd been so active. We lay together in compatible silence, recovering from our efforts, and he began asking about my treatment, its side effects, and how my daily activities were affected. Under normal conditions, during intimate moments, these topics would seem odd to discuss, but Stephen was genuinely curious. Even so, I tried to steer the conversation to Terry, then to Stephen himself.

"You weren't with Terry that long. Did you have any other serious relationships before him?"

"Serious?" He frowned slightly, as if weighing my question. "I suppose so. No one I married, of course, because that's a new right for gays."

"Was there someone you might have made a commitment to at one time? A civil union or a verbal vow?"

"I don't know. I've never really thought about it. Some of my lovers were serious—to use your term—but they only lasted a year or less. A lot of guys disappeared for one reason or the other. I haven't been very lucky in romance, you might say."

"Really? I can't imagine why anyone would leave you."

Stephen smiled and raised his shoulders in a modest shrug. "That's nice of you to say, Bess."

He didn't add details. When he'd said that he disliked the limelight or talking about himself, he had been telling the truth.

He gave me a kiss. "Now, how about I wash the dishes?"

—

I decided to take a shower. In the bathroom, I stared at the deep tub, thinking that getting in and out was more than I could manage. With caution, I eased in, shampooed my hair, toweled off, and returned to the bedroom, wishing I could crawl under the covers and sleep. After resting for a moment, I donned navy shorts and a white blouse and then joined Stephen in the kitchen. He was dressed and had cleaned, dried, and stored all the plates, glasses, and silverware in their proper places. He had also brewed coffee for us and handed me a cup.

"Thank you." I told him. "You're hired."

He chuckled and folded the tea towel over the rod by the sink. "So, what's on for today?"

"First, I have to deal with the divorce papers—sorry." I carried my coffee into the living room, set up the printer, and switched on my laptop. As promised, George had completed the documents. After reading through the pages, I printed and signed them, and Stephen acted as my witness. In anticipation, I'd brought Fed Ex materials. I filled out the mailing information on the airbill, slipped the papers in an envelope, and pulled off the adhesive strip to seal the package.

"Do you want me to take this to a Fed Ex box? I saw one in town."

"Oh, great! That would be very helpful." I quickly checked my inbox and saw emails from Hugh and Nathan, which I decided to read later. Each had also left a message on my cell phone. I didn't listen to either. After turning off the laptop and phone, I said,

"There. Done." Stephen came to sit beside me. He gave me an inquiring look. "Is anything the matter?" I asked.

"Not really. It's just that I'm wondering what we should do. Or rather what I should do…"

"About?"

"About my motel room."

I hesitated for a minute. "About staying there?"

He rubbed his forehead. "Yeah. My room is only reserved until this morning, so I need to decide whether to book another night."

"What are you considering?" Was Stephen about to tell me that he planned to leave Provincetown?

"I don't want to encroach on your private time, Bess, and ordinarily I wouldn't rush a choice like this, but, well, what if I checked out there and checked in here?" He placed a hand on my arm. "Please, if it's an imposition…"

Surprised, I laid my cell phone on the coffee table. "Stephen, can you tell me how you're feeling?" This was evasive, placing the onus on him, yet I felt uncertain about his request and his reasons for prolonging our time together. My suspicions about his "therapizing" our relationship also flared again, though he had been great therapy for me too. And, in truth, his offer made me very happy.

"Hey, I know we just met, but could we simplify things?" he began. "And agree that we enjoy each other's company? That is, unless I'm wrong and you don't want me to stay."

I stared into his light blue eyes. His expression was serene, perhaps even placid, as if he weren't emotionally invested. I wasn't positive this was true.

"I'm not sure we can simplify the situation. I'm worried that you're avoiding being on your own and dealing with your grief." I paused, then added, smiling, "You know I can't stop analyzing, and I know this situation isn't all about you, either. Spending time with you also allows me to avoid facing my problems."

"So, for a short time, maybe being together makes sense…to take a break from our troubles. We might be evading issues, but what's the harm?"

He had a point, yet, as a professional, I knew the rationale wasn't sound. Stephen was looking for a way to shortcut his period of mourning, one that wouldn't advance the process of healing. I sipped some coffee and told him this, gently explaining my point of view.

"Aren't you making an assumption?" he asked. "That I'm using you?"

"You may not even realize it."

"And what about you? Is it the same? I mean, what's wrong with you finding some happiness, even for a little while?"

"Nothing, I suppose. However, my purpose in coming to Provincetown was to make some decisions—"

"You already decided about the divorce."

I nodded. "But I also want to consider how to deal with the future."

"Why can't I help? To listen, to care for you? You're far from home and in pain." Stephen stroked my hand. "I don't want you to be alone, Bess."

His lighter tone had become more solemn. While his words and manner relieved some of my questions about his motives, I was also moved by his genuine expression of concern. "The kindness of strangers," I whispered, half to myself.

Suddenly, a wave of sadness washed over me and mixed with fatigue and the numbing effects of the oxycodone. This blend was insidious, undermining my clarity at a moment when I needed to make the right choice about Stephen. Yet I was clear on one of his points: I had taken a chance driving this distance, although my condition had become more volatile since. Could I trust myself to manage for the next few days? And what about the journey back to Stamford? Coming here had been an exercise in will; returning, was my will sufficient to overcome the incremental impairment I was experiencing?

"Okay," I said, "if this is all right with you, shall we try twenty-four hours together and talk again tomorrow morning?"

"Would you really like that?"

"Yes, Stephen, I would."

"Then that sounds fine."

He leaned over and kissed me. His hand cupped my neck and pulled us together. I felt a quickening of desire, but as I twisted in his embrace, the pain pierced my back. I stiffened.

"What is it, Bess?"

I stroked his cheek and moved away. "I don't know how to say this." I stared at him, overcome with regret. "As much as I liked what we did last night and this morning and will remember both always, well, I'm not up to having sex again." I blew out a lungful of air, surprised at how disappointed I was to make this admission. "Stephen, I've never known such a perfect lover. You were fantastic…the best. So please understand that my decision has nothing to do with you."

He frowned, though I couldn't tell whether he was upset. "Are you positive?"

"Yes." I sighed again, almost ready to rescind my declaration. "I hope this won't matter. I'm really sorry."

I was sorry for me, too, and deflated by the painful acknowledgment that my endurance was so poor. I tipped forward until my head touched Stephen's chest, feeling like my upper body had stumbled, staggered by the weight of all that ailed me. Sometimes, when Hugh was at work, I sat on the edge of the bed, doubled up, as if I'd been seized around the waist with a grip so tight that I couldn't breathe, grasped by the formidable arms of fear. Although Stephen's embrace reduced my anxiety, I still felt battered by frightening thoughts.

"Are you okay?" His voice was a whisper.

"I'm just so tired. I go along fine and then I collapse," I told him. "I don't know whether this is caused by the cancer or the residual effects from chemo."

"Probably both."

"And it's not just lack of energy that's the issue. Whenever I feel happy, a kind of backlash strikes. Like I'm not allowed to experience joy without being assaulted by its opposite. Believe me,

I was never like this before."

"A two-headed coin? Happiness and Sadness?"

I nodded. "I hate how I feel—the weakness, confusion, the conflicts between what my mind wants and what my body is capable of doing. I'm not myself at all. And I'm probably not much fun to be around."

He was silent, which gave me a chance to recover after my confession. I thought of Terry, of Stephen holding him as he held me, and sensed that Terry had wished to disappear into the safety of Stephen's arms as I did now.

Stephen touched my hair. "Hey, who would be a barrel of laughs if they were dealing with cancer?" He gave me a reassuring smile. "Just so you know, Bess, I'm not looking for fun."

—

We talked quietly, trying to regain a more cheerful attitude, which we finally achieved. Once Stephen ascertained that I was okay, he drove to drop the envelope in a Fed Ex box, check out of his motel, and shop for our dinner. I had offered to do the latter, but he insisted I should rest. After he left, I felt a sudden, inexplicable chill, as if his departure had removed the house's warmth. I switched off the air conditioning, opened the windows, and returned to the sofa, where I upbraided myself for succumbing to a bout of depression in front of Stephen, even if my openness had been elicited by his compassion. Instead, I needed to admit how parched I was for emotional sustenance. The closest person in my life—Hugh—only demonstrated shallow sympathy, and my son had been preoccupied with his career and relationship. Colleagues at work had been kind at first, but when I closed my practice and was no longer in the office, they came to the house less and less. Only Susan had listened and shown empathy, but the demands of her work and family limited her free time. With a start, I realized Stephen, during our brief hours together, had relieved my isolation and had granted my unconscious wish for intimate kindness.

I carried my coffee cup into the kitchen, and, after cleaning

Stephen's mug, I heard a car in the drive. It was too soon for Stephen to return, but perhaps he'd forgotten something. I walked to the front door, opened it, and saw a taxi. Then a man stepped out.

"Nathan!" I cried.

I ran down the sidewalk and threw my arms around my son. He was taller than Hugh, about the same height as Stephen, but more slender than both, having inherited my build. For a moment, as I hugged him, I worried about telling Nathan about Stephen and felt a twinge of disloyalty to Hugh. My son was aware of Hugh's affairs and probably wouldn't disapprove of my infidelity, at least in theory; in practice, Nathan might strenuously disapprove.

"Hi, Mom." He gave me a boyish, uneven smile.

"What are you doing here?"

"Didn't you get my phone messages and emails?"

"Yes, but I didn't listen to them or read my emails."

I'd told Nathan where I was staying in case of an emergency but given strict instructions not to tell his father. I had no worry that he would because Nathan wasn't close to Hugh, especially since my diagnosis, when the two had argued bitterly. Nathan was furious that Hugh had missed taking me to several chemo appointments, and I'd had to drive myself. But his difficulties with Hugh had started during Nathan's childhood and had escalated into an attitude just short of outright animosity.

"Oh, but it doesn't matter," I added. "I'm so glad to see you! Come inside."

"Sure, let me get my things." He paid the cab driver, handed me a bag containing four bottles of wine, and removed a navy duffel, leather briefcase, and raincoat from the back seat.

"Where's your car?"

"I left it in the city, took the train to Boston and a ferry to Provincetown last night. It was late so I thought I'd wait to arrive this morning."

"And Melissa didn't come with you?" Melissa was Nathan's girlfriend.

"No, but that's okay." He glanced away when he said this.

I didn't pursue the matter because Nathan's evasiveness indicated something was wrong between the two of them, which he had implied during our last phone conversations. We hurried inside, where Nathan admired the broad floorboards, the white plaster walls, and the view through the large windows. I set the wine on the table and showed him into the guest bedroom, whose ceiling was low. As Stephen had done in the kitchen, Nathan tilted his head.

"This place must be old," he said, lifting his duffel bag onto one of the twin beds. "Except for the raised roof over the living room and the new windows."

"The original house—the living room and powder room— was built in the early 1800s, according to the owners. The outer wings were added later, before the center area was modernized. Thankfully, at that time, central air conditioning was installed." I pointed to the small circular ducts set into the upper walls.

"Glad they did, especially in this weather."

As Nathan unzipped his bag, I admired my son, who looked neat in pressed tan chinos and a starched gold-and-white checked shirt. Unlike the last time I'd seen him, when he'd been sporting a mustache, today Nathan was clean shaven, which I preferred. And despite living and working in Manhattan, his face was freshly tan due to a recent outing in the sun. He was more handsome than ever.

While Nathan hung up his clothes, I went into the kitchen to make coffee. As I set the black kettle on the stove, I wondered what to tell Nathan about Stephen, who would most likely arrive within an hour or so. Should I be truthful about what happened between us? I'd never found myself in this kind of quandary before, having never cheated on Hugh or been deceptive with my son except to shield him from his father's affairs during Nathan's early years. When he learned later what a philanderer his father was, he had been furious at Hugh, but he was also angry that I'd papered over the rot, hiding the truth from him. Even so, Nathan had quickly and wholeheartedly aligned with me. But would he accept what I'd just done? Although I felt emotionally free because of the impending divorce, I had always held myself to high standards and couldn't shake feeling guilty. And how would Stephen react to the sudden insertion of Nathan when he expected us to be alone? Would he be disappointed? What was I supposed to say to him about the sleeping arrangements? Bunk in the guest room with my son?

Nathan entered the kitchen and admired the rustic farm table, whose surface green paint had been lightly whitewashed. He ran his craftsman's hands over the top. "Nice job."

During high school, for two summers, he had apprenticed with a building and furniture restorer. This experience had sparked his interest in architecture, which began with the antique and had expanded into the contemporary.

He sat on the chair by the window while I poured his coffee—black, because he preferred to taste the flavor, or so he had decided at age fourteen. In this and in many things, Nathan's choices in clothes, furniture, cars, and artwork were simple, utilitarian, but elegant. He liked lean lines, perhaps because his body was constructed that way, yet he also appreciated handmade objects and old houses such as this cottage.

After slipping his long fingers through the mug's pistol grip, he lifted the cup to his mouth, squinted slightly because the liquid was hot, and swallowed. I topped off my own mug and tried to sort out the best way to explain what had occurred during the last twenty-four hours.

"So, Mom, how are you feeling?" He looked at me closely. His eyes were amber-brown. Sometimes, in sunlight, they glinted with gold.

I started to say "fine" and stopped myself. I needed to be honest. "Up and down. The pain is worse. Consistently so." I stirred my coffee. "It was probably foolish to drive here, but I needed to think."

"About Dad?" Nathan guessed.

I nodded. "You know we've had a history of problems—"

"Yeah, he causes them and you deal with them."

"That may be true," I agreed, "but I just took action and called my attorney. He emailed divorce papers, which I signed and returned overnight express. Hugh will receive a letter of intent in a day or two, asking him to leave the house." Nathan ran his fingers through his curly copper-colored hair, which was exactly the same shade as my father's, and stared at his coffee, his brow lightly furrowed. "Nathan, are you upset about my decision?"

He leaned against his chair, causing its old wood to creak. "Mom, you should have done this years ago. I'm just sorry that it's happening now when Dad might be useful." Nathan thought about this for a minute before adding, "But he's not very dependable."

"No, he isn't. I understand your concern for my welfare, and, honestly, I'm concerned too. Yes, you're right, this isn't the most opportune time to separate, but I can't tolerate the deceit any longer. I need to draw the line, to firmly end our marriage."

I proceeded to lay out my rationale, watching his reaction closely, and noting that while he was with me in principle, nodding here and there, Nathan's frown deepened as I continued. Was he running through ways he could help? If so, how much would I let him? He was thirty-six-years old, residing in New York City, with a demanding full-time job, and had been dating Melissa exclusively for almost a year, a relationship that seemed to require a lot of his attention.

"I'm sorry if this comes as a shock," I apologized.

"It does and it doesn't. Have you told Dad that you're sending the papers?"

I shook my head. "It's cowardly not to confront him in person, but I can't deal with a lengthy, pointless harangue. I'm sure he'll telephone and try to talk me out of a divorce—"

"Unless he's shacked up with someone." A flash of contempt crossed his face.

"I doubt that he is." In truth, I had no idea what Hugh was doing in my absence.

Nathan said nothing, but his expression appeared skeptical, either of his father or of my naïve belief in Hugh.

I finished drinking my coffee and peeked at my watch. Though I didn't know when Stephen would return, it could be very soon.

"Nathan, I have something else to tell you."

8

My son looked different from when I'd seen him a few weeks ago. Regardless of the healthy tan, he appeared older, as if he'd aged several years. There were new lines on his forehead, between his eyes and at his mouth, and, unless I was mistaken, his posture was deflated: head bowed slightly forward, shoulders drawn together. Was Nathan unhappy? He'd intimated that he and Melissa were having some issues. I hoped not, because she was a lovely woman who seemed like a perfect match for him. Or was Nathan dissatisfied with his career as an architect? From early days playing with Lincoln logs and constructing forts, he had always been passionate about building things, culminating in a great position with a firm that specialized in large commercial projects. I would ask about what was troubling him, but first I needed to explain about Stephen, since he might arrive momentarily.

Nathan cocked his head. "What is it, Mom?"

"Well, yesterday I spent the afternoon at the ocean. On the National Seashore," I began. "I saw a man swimming and noticed two sharks coming toward him."

"Oh, my god! What did you do?"

"I yelled. Luckily, he heard me and rushed safely to shore."

"That's good."

"Yes, it was," I replied. "Anyhow, we started talking."

Nathan pulled away from me, an almost infinitesimal half

inch, but I noticed it.

"And then what happened?"

"We sat on the beach for a while and were enjoying our conversation so I invited him for dinner. As it turns out, Stephen is gay and has just lost his husband to leukemia this spring."

"And you put on your therapist's hat?" He gave me a little smile—this was a teasing remark he often made.

"In a way, yes, but in a way, no, I didn't. Remember that I'm retired—or I'm trying to be. This means not being the world's perpetual caretaker."

Nathan chuckled. "When you stop doing that, I'll go into shock."

I acknowledged his point with a nod. "I know. But I don't have the balance to be a therapist any longer—I'm too unstable. Worrying about my health and dealing with the effects of chemo." I paused for a moment. "And I've come to realize something else. By placing myself in this part all the time, it means other people can't give to me because they can't get past my imposed boundaries—which were necessary in my practice. Not now."

"Yeah, that's true, Mom."

"Well, over the last two days I've concluded that I must change. Especially toward those people close to me—you in particular. I need to be more open about how I'm feeling, share more rather than pretend everything is okay, like I did with Hugh all these years. The divorce is symbolic, I suppose. I'm divorcing my husband but also divorcing my career and some of my old behaviors." I reached across the table and took his hand. "Nathan, I hope we can enter a new kind of relationship, one in which we can really talk to each other. Not so much as mother and son…more as equals, as friends."

"Sure." He curled his fingers around mine. "I'm good with that."

"Fine. I'll count on you to tell me when I'm falling into old habits, okay?"

"Okay. So what about this guy Stephen? Did you have dinner?"

I let go of his hand and tried to reconcile my reluctance to explain what happened versus my pledge to be more truthful. "Yes, we had a very special time. He talked to me about his partner, Terry, and how painful it's been these last months. Stephen is extremely handsome, and he believes people don't take his grief seriously because they think he can replace Terry without any effort."

"That's an odd prejudice."

"It is," I said, nodding. "I also told him about what I've been experiencing the last months."

Nathan's eyes narrowed, as if he felt jealous that I'd confided in a stranger rather than in him. Then he took a last sip of coffee and abruptly stood. "Hold on, Mom. Got to run to the head."

I was glad for a reprieve, a chance to consider how to approach my confession. I brought our coffee cups to the sink, washed and dried them, and leaned against the counter, staring out the window. A blue jay zipped into an pine tree and began uttering a combination of soft gurgling sounds with those that were harsh, like a miniature pile driver. A breeze shuddered the green leaves and drifted in through the open window, bringing with it the acrid scent of oak and the fainter smell of salt water. In another two months, autumn would change the view, and I wouldn't be here in this snug cottage to witness it. And, as always when I thought about time, I wondered how many more seasons I would experience. Another winter? Another spring?

But today was a fine day, one to celebrate. I wiped my hands on a towel and, seeking to increase the circulation through the house, walked into the living room to unlatch the top part of the Dutch door. Just then, the door flew open and in came Stephen, his arms full of groceries. He gave me an enormous smile, placed the bags on the sofa, and pulled me into an embrace.

"Oh, Bess! I missed you!" He laughed. "Isn't that crazy?"

At that moment, Nathan entered the room. He had changed into khaki shorts and was tucking in his shirt. When he saw Stephen, he stopped and his face froze. Stephen turned quickly, equally stunned to find company.

I gasped and disengaged from Stephen. Both men were staring at each other—Nathan with a protective bearing and Stephen with curiosity.

"Stephen, this is my son, Nathan Lynch-Chatham."

"Hi, I'm Stephen Andersen." He crossed the space between them. "Nice to meet you."

Stephen offered his hand and Nathan shook it, glancing at me as he did, obviously trying to work out the implications of the comments and the intimate hug.

I exhaled slowly. "We'll discuss everything in a minute, Nathan. Let's get things sorted."

Stephen gazed at me, still bewildered, but a trace of amusement was rising behind the confusion. He started to say something and didn't. Instead, he grabbed the groceries and headed for the kitchen.

Nathan walked to my side. "What's going on, Mother?" he whispered.

"I'm sorry. I was about to tell you when…oh, what a mess!"

"How much of a mess is it?" he demanded.

"I don't know." I placed my hand on my forehead and sighed. "Stephen and I had dinner and were talking—like I said. I certainly didn't expect anything more than a pleasant evening, but when we began sharing our problems, we connected. It was a total surprise. I mean, Stephen is gay, after all…or bisexual."

In the kitchen, Stephen was opening the refrigerator and unpacking the groceries. He could hear our conversation. What was he thinking? Did he believe I'd known about Nathan's visit and not told him? That my decision to stop having sex was because of my son's arrival?

"So then what?" Nathan already knew the answer, but his lips were twitching, a telltale sign of annoyance that I recognized from his childhood. It was clear that he wanted me to admit the truth despite my obvious embarrassment, but whether he was jealous of Stephen, apprehensive about my welfare, or merely thrown off balance, I had no idea.

I touched his shoulder. "Nathan, you know I've never betrayed your father."

"Yes."

"Well, last night—although it hadn't been my plan—I did. I can't explain why except to say that Stephen is a very kind, very caring—"

"Hunk." Nathan stepped away and dropped down on the sofa, as if that statement had felled him.

I sat beside my son. "Yes, he's handsome, but that had nothing to do with it." I wanted to move closer yet didn't want to crowd Nathan as he digested the news. "In fact, I told Stephen this morning that we could no longer continue physically. I can't deal with it on a lot of levels."

His face relaxed a little, as if this decision mollified his displeasure. In a low tone, so Stephen couldn't hear, he asked, "How'd he take it?"

I sighed again, relieved that Nathan was coming around. "Fine. He left to go shopping a few minutes later and to…"

"And to what?"

"To check out of his motel."

He opened his mouth in astonishment. "Huh? He's staying here? With us?"

I nodded. I felt my face flush. At that moment, Stephen appeared in the doorway. He hesitated before walking closer.

"Nathan, if you're unhappy about having me here, that's okay. I understand you came to be with Bess and that it's important for the two of you to have a private visit." He placed his hands in his pockets. "I can return to the motel—no problem."

Nathan stared at him and at me.

"It's up to you, Nathan," I said. "Your call."

My son came to his feet and focused on Stephen. For a second, I thought he would insist that Stephen leave immediately. There was starch in his bearing, a proprietary attitude that I'd never seen before, as if he were standing in for Hugh or defending the family's reputation. As well as I knew him, I couldn't tell what he would say.

"I don't know," Nathan began. He shifted his stance from one foot to the other, and with it, I hoped, his decision. "You're right, I was planning on being with my mother. By ourselves."

"I'll leave then," Stephen offered.

His willingness to do so made Nathan reconsider. He cupped his hand around his neck and rested it there, a habit he had copied from his father. "Well, if Mom and I have some time together this afternoon, I don't care about later…dinner and…"

"Thanks," Stephen said. "I'll head over to the ocean for a few hours. Would that work?"

Nathan nodded and finally smiled. "Yeah. That's fine, I guess."

Relief swept over me. The last thing I wanted was discord with my son or with Stephen. "Nathan, we'll manage. I promise. We have a lot to talk about."

He gave me an uncertain look, either because he still wasn't sure about Stephen's presence or because he had something else on his mind that was making him feel uneasy. He touched the top of the chair, smoothing the slipcovers. "Okay."

Nathan wasn't absolutely settled, but the sooner Stephen was on his way to the beach, the sooner my son and I could deal with his distress. In a voice that aimed at enthusiasm, I suggested we eat lunch on the patio.

Nathan agreed and started walking to the kitchen. As he passed Stephen, Stephen began to pat him on the shoulder but stopped, perhaps believing that this familiarity was premature and would be unwelcome.

"Would you guys get the seat cushions?" I pointed to the closet next to the kitchen. "And set the table?"

—

Because of the roof's overhang, the green wrought-iron table was mostly in shade except for one side. Stephen and I opted to stay out of the sun, near the house, but Nathan chose to sit in sunlight, fully illuminated. Behind him, the garden sparkled with blue delphiniums, pink phlox, yellow snapdragons, purple salvias, and assorted herbs, all which I'd watered on my arrival.

Thankfully, most of the earlier awkwardness had dissipated, and Nathan seemed easier about our arrangement. In fact, unless I was mistaken, I noticed that he glanced at Stephen on occasion, probably as dazed by this embodiment of perfection as I was. Because my son always had issues with socially adept men such as his father and tended to become withdrawn in their presence, I was curious as to how Nathan would behave around Stephen. I was glad to see that Stephen was friendly but not intrusive, that he maintained a deferential pose and steered the conversation in Nathan's direction, which seemed to suit my son.

"What kind of work do you do? Stephen asked.

Nathan ate a large bite of lobster salad. "I'm a commercial architect in Manhattan."

"Wow! That's impressive!"

Nathan nodded and drank some red wine that he'd brought. "Yeah, well, I love the work but not where I work."

I noticed the downcast tone and was instantly worried. "Oh? What's going on?"

"I was going to tell you later, Mom." He poured himself more wine and then ran a finger over the green and mauve placemat. "As of Friday, I'm officially unemployed. Cutbacks."

"No! I'm so sorry!" I laid my hand on his. "You've worked so hard!"

"I have. The company fired the three most junior employees, and I was the third. They gave me a financial package that should last while I look for another job."

"Sorry to hear your news, Nathan," Stephen said. "That's rough."

"It is, but actually this might be a good thing. It means I can be home to help you more often," he said to me. "And with this divorce, well, I can take up a little of the slack." He gave a small snort, no doubt because of his reference to Hugh's absentee behavior.

"That's wonderful, dear. I would really appreciate that. However,

I don't want you to jeopardize your job search or your relationship with Melissa. You have a life to live."

"And so do you," Nathan replied, dipping his head in acknowledgment. "At the moment, your life is more important than mine."

I started to disagree and glanced at Stephen. A slow smile of approval was spreading across his face.

—

After lunch, Stephen offered to buy a third steak and potato for dinner, explaining that he'd purchased charcoal earlier and was planning to cook the meal in the domed grill outside. He left for the beach, and Nathan and I remained on the patio, talking, but soon the metal seat became uncomfortable. The oxycodone had worn off. I needed more pain medication and not pills.

"Would you stick a fentanyl patch on my back?"

"When did you start using it?" Nathan asked.

"A long while ago." He had forgotten about the fentanyl, which I'd told him about. "It's more effective than taking pills every six hours and provides continuous relief."

"Is it stronger?"

"Yes, but it doesn't affect me too much. I've become acclimated." I hoped this would also be true of a double dose.

We walked into my bedroom, and I removed a sealed envelope from the box. "Apply the patch above the scapula, on the flat area where there is minimal movement, and hold your hand on it for a minute so the heat makes the adhesive stick." I unbuttoned the top of my blouse and exposed the upper section of my back.

"But you already have one on."

"I know. Just add the second patch on the other side." After my arrival in Truro, I had placed one there with difficulty because I preferred not to have the patch show in front.

Nathan followed instructions and didn't ask about the dosage change. His lack of curiosity and his self-preoccupation reminded me of Hugh. I put this unhappy comparison aside.

"There you go." He patted my shoulder, hesitated, and then gave me a hug. "Mom, I know I haven't been the best son recently. Things will be different. I promise."

I was touched. Nathan wasn't demonstrative so this embrace carried meaning. "You've had a lot on your mind. I've been managing well so far." I paused, remembering my vow to be truthful. "But I'm concerned about how long I'll be so independent. I'm even losing more weight."

He drew away and examined me at arm's length. "A little, maybe. Not much. I'm sure you're doing fine."

"It's not easy to eat sometimes, but, yes, I'm all right." I felt a small wave of sadness, aroused by Nathan's inattentiveness. "Now, let me make a note about the fentanyl on my calendar or I'll forget."

—

In the kitchen, Nathan replenished the wine in his glass, and I poured more water for myself. We moved into the living room, and I turned on the air-conditioner and closed the windows. Nathan selected the armchair on the left, the one mostly in shadow, as if he preferred to be less visible now compared to earlier on the patio. He lowered himself into it, folding his knees in front of the rectangular coffee table, and rested the wine glass on his thigh. As before, he appeared pulled in on himself. Something beside my welfare was worrying him.

I stretched out on the sofa. My back still throbbed, but perhaps in a few minutes it would hurt less. "So, tell me how you are."

"I'm okay," he said. "Losing my job was really a shock."

"I can imagine it must have been devastating even though you had a little warning. As I recall, the last time we spoke you mentioned this might happen. That rumors were going around that the company needed to cut overhead expenses."

"Yeah, I thought they'd stop buying flowers for the lobby and giving us free doughnuts. Silly me."

He used this sardonic tone when he wasn't happy, to deflect

from his true emotional reaction. Ever since he'd been a child, Nathan tended to be reserved, awkward about expressing his feelings. From time to time, he would allow me to come close, providing that I wasn't too inquisitive, and if I approached in a manner that matched his mood, if I could smoothly synchronize our gears. Never would he confide in his father, but then again, Hugh seldom tried to communicate with Nathan except for hearty, one-sided, father-son discourses on how Nathan could improve his personality, grades, athletic skills, or success with girls.

I smiled to acknowledge his remark, yet I wanted to keep the conversation on a serious track and not be sidelined by his attempt at bleak humor. I asked him about the termination, where he might look for another position, and how he felt about this change in his life. Nathan listed firms where he'd already submitted inquiries, several of which were in the city, but two were located in Stamford and one in New Haven.

"I applied to some places near home so I could be closer," he said.

"I really appreciate that, Nathan, but you need to select the best opportunity for you. A company where you can grow and your talent will be appreciated."

"Yeah. Well, we'll see how it all works out. Perhaps I'll get lucky."

He then fell silent. Not sullen or resistant, as he sometimes could be. Just quiet, involved with his thoughts.

I hoped he would say more, but he didn't. Changing the subject, I asked, "And Melissa? What's going on with her?"

Nathan shifted his gaze to the window and drummed his fingers on the arms of the chair, thus telegraphing why he was depressed.

Melissa was the central problem.

9

~~~~~~

Nathan glowered at his wine glass, ran his finger around its rim, and took a large swallow. I wasn't sure if he was annoyed by my question or whether he was too distressed to answer.

"Melissa called it quits," he said at last. "After eleven months of living together."

"Oh, Nathan! I'm so sorry!"

"Yeah, me too," he said.

"Is that what you wanted or was this her decision?"

"Mostly hers. Or at least she was the one who ended it. I don't know if I would have stayed with Melissa anyway." Nathan shrugged, as if he didn't care.

I'd seen that gesture too many times to believe him. "Did you have an argument? Or did something happen?"

"Yeah. We had several arguments over the last month." He nodded but didn't look at me. "I really cared about her, though. But…"

"But?"

"But she wasn't right."

"I know you believed she was, in the beginning. Very smart and attractive, you told me on the phone. Remember? And when I met Melissa, I agreed. You seemed like a great match," I said with sincere regret.

I thought about his dating history, which, considering his looks and intelligence, was sparse. As soon as Nathan was a freshman in high school, Hugh had pushed him to invite girls to dances. Nathan usually refused, as he refused to follow most of his father suggestions, an automatic resistance that usually produced heated words on both sides. It didn't help that my son was shy, more like me, and very unlike Hugh, who gravitated toward the center of any gathering. Not until college did Nathan date anyone seriously. And perhaps he did then because he was in California and out of range of his father's scrutiny.

Hoping to encourage a fuller recounting, I added, "Sometimes things change."

"They do." He twisted in his chair. "Well, whatever might have been between us is now finished. After I leave here, I'll pick up my clothes at her apartment. I would have packed before coming, but I wanted to get away. Clear my head." His voice dropped to a whisper, as if discouragement blunted the volume.

Nathan hadn't explained why Melissa had concluded their relationship or why he was suddenly ambivalent about her. I hesitated to ask because I rarely intervened in my son's life, doing so only when necessary. Was this such a time? I weighed my wish to know against his privacy and compromised. "I know you're hurting. This must be a big blow even if the two of you were having difficulties."

His eyes briefly held mine. I detected a tiny crack in his stoicism, out of which emerged the image of a little boy who ran to me when he was upset, circled his arms around my neck, and pressed his wet cheek against mine. A flood of compassion spread over me, the maternal kind that differed from the professional sympathy I felt for my clients.

"It's been a rotten week," he said, "but I'm glad to be here. And, of course, mostly I wanted to see you."

"That makes me happy." I smiled at my son, wanting to say more but deciding to wait for him to continue.

Nathan's expression brightened. "You know I'd do anything for you. Anything. In fact, one of the reasons I came was to tell you that." He said this with conviction, as if he'd been holding in this avowal until the most opportune moment arose. "And, since I no longer need to be in New York except for some job interviews over the next few weeks, I was thinking about returning home. If that's okay."

I was deeply moved by his offer and very relieved. "I'd love nothing more." Tears welled up in my eyes. My son saw them and kneeled on the carpet in front of the couch. I leaned forward, and he took my hands in his.

"I've been so preoccupied, Mom, but it's felt like everything was falling apart," he said. "Still, that's no excuse for not helping."

"Nathan, I knew you were dealing with a lot of problems."

"I still should have been there with you." He gripped my hands more firmly, for emphasis. "I guess I was afraid."

"That's normal...to be afraid. What I'm going through is frightening. The unknown always is." Though in my case the unknown was limited to time rather than the conclusion. I didn't mention this to Nathan.

"I regret these last months, Mom. Particularly when Dad let you down." His mouth tightened. "And speaking of Dad, he was why I didn't visit often. We always have trouble relating, but I was worried that I'd really lose it with him. On the other hand, considering how I've behaved, being mad at Dad for abandoning you is sort of hypocritical."

"It's okay. My illness has put the three of us in a pressure cooker, where all the old conflicts heat up and intensify. We're not ourselves."

"Maybe so." He let go of my hand and returned to his chair. "The other problem with Dad is that he criticizes me all the time." Nathan exhaled slowly. "When I don't succeed—in his mind, on his terms. Like the relationship with Melissa. He'd view that failure as all my fault. And even if it might be mostly my fault, I don't need to hear it from him." He thought for a moment and continued. "Oh, yeah, Dad might commiserate a little at first: 'That's too bad, Nathan. So sorry, Son,' but pretty soon that would change to:

'Why'd you let Melissa get away? What's wrong with you?' And the situation at work? Even though the decision was based on seniority and not merit, he'd turn that around so that I screwed up."

"Hugh is not always sympathetic."

Nathan snorted. "An understatement! He's never cared about how I feel. Remember when I didn't want to play baseball, but he got it into his head that I should become a pitcher? Because I'm a lefty?"

"I do. You were nine, I think."

"Yeah. Every night he'd make me throw a hundred pitches at that goddamned target in the backyard. You know? The guy holding a bat that Dad painted on a sheet of plywood?"

I could easily visualize the grotesque clown-like figure. Hugh had worked late at night in the garage, sawing and painting, excited about surprising Nathan. He had been crushed by Nathan's hostile reaction.

"Your father cut a big hole in the batter's chest where the strike zone was supposed to be. So you could throw the balls inside."

"And the damned thing was wearing a Red Sox cap! I hated that team, and Dad knew it." Nathan shook his head in disgust. "Even when my arm hurt, he didn't care. Dad said I was acting like a baby, that I needed to toughen up."

I nodded. "I took you to the doctor's. You had shoulder tendonitis."

"What a fight that was when you told Dad to stop making me pitch! He accused you of—what was the word he used? Oh, yeah, mollycoddling me."

This was only one of many father-son battles, some of which I tried to mediate, usually without success. It almost seemed that whatever Hugh cared about, Nathan rejected, and whatever Nathan enjoyed, Hugh denigrated. "I think Hugh wanted you to be like him," I said. "Most fathers feel that way."

Nathan grunted in response.

"Your father had fixed ideas about how boys should behave based on how he was raised."

"And that turned out brilliantly," Nathan scoffed.

"I hadn't realized you felt so angry with him," I said gently.

"Don't give me that shrink talk! Of course, I'm fucking angry!" He blinked after uttering the profanity, one Hugh didn't allow in our house. "The way he's treated both of us…with his stupid affairs and now…"

"This might sound like I'm excusing your father—I'm not—but he's done the best he can. Being empathetic isn't comfortable for him—"

"Stop it! Dad's an asshole!"

I eased against my chair. "Yes, Nathan. Sometimes he is." I looked at my son, hoping to see his scowl lighten. After it did, I continued. "When he should show caring, well, Hugh runs away. His relationship with his mother was probably to blame. She treated Hugh like a deity but also demanded his attention. Kind of a mixed signal, pushing him out the door to display his superiority and pulling him back, making Hugh feel guilty for abandoning her. He conflated someone needing him with being smothered. Escape became the safest route."

"Or taking complete control and telling everyone what to do," he muttered. "I didn't like Grandma. She was always hugging and kissing me and—oh—the worst! Pinching my cheek?"

"You did have cute cheeks," I said, covering my smile.

"Mom!" Nathan mock-protested. "God! I hated that!"

"I asked her not to do it."

"Didn't stop her, though. Then, after Grandma finished torturing my face, she'd give me the once-over. 'Oh, he's going to be a lady-killer when he grows up.' I bet she told Dad the same thing when he was little."

"She probably did. Even so, she adored you," I said. "Like she did your father." I reflected for a minute. "I never felt Hugh loved me as much as he loved his mother. They had a formidable bond despite how often she irritated him."

Nathan mused on this. "I wish your mother was still alive. She was cool."

"I wish she was around too." How many times I'd dreamed that my mother hadn't died, that she could take care of me when I was suffering after chemo or was feeling afraid of dying or was confused about complex medical issues. I missed her acutely, now more than ever. "One of these days, Nathan, you may come to see your father in a different light. When—"

"He's all the family I have left?"

I hadn't meant to lead him to that conclusion, although that's what I was thinking. "You'll make your own family."

Nathan shook his head. "I don't think so."

"Yes, you will! A great woman is waiting in the wings. I'm sure of it."

He didn't answer me. I couldn't tell whether he was still smarting about Melissa or whether he was discouraged about his ability to manage a primary relationship. "You're such a wonderful guy. Someone will come along."

"Someone might, maybe."

Nathan was only saying this to appease my concern. He didn't sound at all convinced. Because I began dating Hugh in my early twenties, I'd never really undergone a period of doubt as to whether I'd marry—plenty of doubts about staying married, however. And my mother had been alive to lend support during the turbulent years with Hugh, even with the demands of her pediatric practice. Nathan wouldn't be so fortunate, an awareness that cut me with sharp grief. If only my son's circumstances were different, with aunts and uncles and cousins to provide a family; because Hugh and I had no siblings and our parents were deceased, Nathan would be on his own unless he reconciled with his father. Although I'd agonized about my son before, this idea struck with fresh potency now that Melissa was out of the picture.

"Nathan, I hope you'll try to repair the rift between you and your father. Regardless of what you think of him, Hugh is upset about me and will be shaken when he receives the divorce notification. Please promise that you'll be kind to him. He does love you and is very proud of you."

Nathan frowned, about to protest, but finally acquiesced. "Okay, Mom. I'll try."

"I appreciate it. I'll feel better knowing that you'll make an effort. And, if all goes as I've asked, Hugh won't be in the house when I return—when we return—so you won't have to deal with him for the present unless you wish to do so."

"And if he doesn't leave?"

I shrugged. "Let's see what my attorney can arrange and trust that your father will do the right thing."

"I suppose I can talk with Dad if that doesn't work. He's not going to pick a fight when you're having chemo, which is soon, isn't it?"

"Possibly next week. If the platelet numbers have risen."

He gave me a blank look. "What does that mean?"

"In early June, I had to skip several infusions because the bloodwork indicated a low platelet count, which can be dangerous. Thrombocytopenia can cause spontaneous internal bleeding, for example. Dr. Melbourne warned me that this could prove to be a significant impediment."

"Why?"

"Because the current chemo mixture was working miraculously well and can't be continued unless the platelets remain at a safe number. Another combination of drugs might be possible to try, but they're an older and less effective treatment."

"I thought you were already in remission. Aren't you?"

I was surprised that Nathan had misunderstood the reasons for the hiatus from chemo. I'd taken particular care to explain the matter clearly. "No, I'm not in remission. Since the MRIs have been stable, I was given time off to recover and to allow the platelets to normalize so that we might keep going with the original regimen." I paused, worried that my son wasn't comprehending the gravity of my illness. "Nathan, as I've said before, a complete remission is extremely unlikely. Not with Stage IV pancreatic cancer. And the last MRI was done in May. No one knows what's happened over the summer." I kept my voice measured, but I didn't feel calm.

"When I return to Stamford, I'm scheduled for a CT scan and then, a few days later, an appointment with Dr. Melbourne and chemo. The following week, I see the doctor in New York. As you know, Dr. Melbourne has been consulting with her whenever a decision is required."

"Is there one? A decision?"

"Well, if the platelet count stays low or drops again after the infusion, there's discussion about a partial splenectomy. Tying off a section of the spleen, which is sequestering the platelets. The idea is that this will free the platelets so I can continue with treatment. The trick is deciding when to do the surgery. If the bloodwork is okay when I see Dr. Melbourne, we'll proceed with the same chemo mixture—the longer we can do this, the better. On the other hand, if the platelets are low, the splenectomy might be necessary, though a low platelet count can also complicate surgery. Kind of a quintessential Catch-22 problem," I said. "At any rate, the doctors will confer, and we'll see what the consensus is."

Nathan frowned. "That sounds like a big deal. With the spleen."

"Yes, it might be." I sighed. I wanted to tell him that other frightening possibilities existed, but he would learn these for himself if he did some homework. "Are you planning to come to my next appointment with Dr. Melbourne?"

"Oh, yeah, I am."

"Good. You can read my past test results and some articles I've copied so you're prepared. And we should have the CT scan information by the time we see her," I told him. "But, Nathan, my status might change. Although the chemo has kept the tumors in check so far, I've been extraordinarily fortunate. The scan may show new tumor enlargement and spread." I saw the concern in his eyes and wished I could avoid saying anything more. Yet he'd demonstrated some unwillingness to face realistic truths, which I'd painstakingly set out from the beginning. "Few people live as long as I have. The likelihood is that the primary pancreatic tumor will begin metastasizing more rapidly as will the tumors in my liver, if they haven't done so already. And the spleen situation might become precarious."

He nodded, his face grave. "Mom, I'll be with you during your next visit, and I'll drive you into the city. I also promise to do more research so I understand what's happening. My days of sitting on the bench are over."

"Thank you, Nathan. I really mean that." I hesitated for a second, then asked, "Have you made a decision about having the genetic testing? If you want, we can schedule this for the same day as my consultation in the city."

"I've thought about it. I know I have a fifty-fifty chance of inheriting that BRCA2 gene." He looked away from me. "I'm not sure I want to find out."

"It might help for your doctor to screen more aggressively for the three cancers associated with the mutation. Early detection is really important."

"Yeah. We'll see."

—

We made two cups of Darjeeling tea and sat at the dining table, playing backgammon. It had been many years since Nathan and I had done this, and it felt just right. I imagined we might do this more often when I became sicker, or we might play two-handed euchre or rummy as we had during hot summer afternoons on the screened-in porch when Nathan was a boy. I remembered how small his hands were then, as they grasped the cards, holding a large fan of them with difficulty.

As nostalgic as I was for my child and his sweet innocence, I was glad my son was an adult, able to face the coming months with me when I transformed from being his mother into being a woman he scarcely recognized. It distressed me terribly to picture that transformation, the loss of dignity and independence, the growing inability to remain his chief supporter, and, most painfully, to realize I wouldn't be present to console Nathan after I died.

I stared at his long fingers, with their prominent knuckles, at the gold signet ring of my father's, which Nathan had worn since high school, and hoped he was as strong as his hands appeared. Was he prepared for what would occur, especially if I declined over many months rather than dying swiftly? I'd taken care of my mother in hospice, at home, and knew how grindingly difficult the end stage could be, especially dealing with the physical indignities that had embarrassed my mother and would definitely embarrass me. My plan was to hire round-the-clock aides when it became necessary, but Nathan would be required to provide hands-on help some of the time.

As much as I wanted to spare Nathan this terrible experience, the only way to do it was to put an end to my life. Would that be harder or easier for him to handle? Could I actually commit suicide? I held no moral or religious compunctions about the matter and firmly supported the right of dying people to make this decision. Even so, I felt a deep hesitancy about taking a handful of pills. Was I a coward or in a state of partial denial like my son? Clinging to an irrational belief that medical science or my body could defeat the cancer and restore my health? Probably everyone with this disease held some secret optimism, desperately grasping for any shred of hope.

I leaned against my chair, determined to put away these thoughts and revel in Nathan's presence. I loved being in his company, loved admiring my son's neatly cut, wavy hair and clean looks. When I'd told him that he would soon find another woman to date, I wasn't exaggerating.

"Mom, you're awfully quiet," Nathan said, throwing the dice. "Are you worrying about that guy? Stephen?"

I didn't want to discuss Stephen because I didn't know how I felt about him. "No, not at all. Sometimes, I have these small walkabouts." I smiled at Nathan. "Actually, I was just thinking what a fine man you've become. I said earlier that your father is very proud of you, but so am I."

"Come on, you're trying to distract me from winning!"

He gave me a big grin.

—

Nathan won two out of three games of backgammon and gloated a little, almost giggling with pleasure. "It's been ages since I've played."

"Yes, it has. We didn't have as much time together once I began working full time."

"Which meant I was stuck with Dad and baseball, football, and basketball. Ugh, how I hated all that!"

"I thought you liked basketball." I said. "And running."

"I liked shooting hoops with the guys, not with Dad. Track?" He laughed. "I liked running because Dad didn't and couldn't."

Hugh had always been stocky and had gained weight during Nathan's early years. Though Hugh was a fine golfer and could play catch with Nathan, jogging was not a sport he undertook.

"No, he hated anything aerobic," I said. "Even swimming."

Nathan chuckled. "You and I loved the water. Going to the pool. And on weeks during the summer, at the shore, swimming in the ocean."

I smiled. "I remember the pink Victorian house we rented for several years."

"Across from the beach. The place with the turrets and the purple shutters? Yeah, that was great. And the best part was that Dad usually stayed home."

I didn't respond to Nathan's remark, though I agreed with him.

We closed the backgammon set and then heard Stephen's car in the drive. Nathan stood, slipped the game into the cupboard, and turned to look at me. I could tell he was suppressing a comment about Stephen, but he walked to the half-open Dutch door and greeted Stephen as he approached.

10

Stephen entered with the groceries and his straw bag. His face was slightly flushed, though, as yesterday, considering the number of hours he'd been at the beach, it was surprising that his skin wasn't redder. Next to my tall son, Stephen appeared larger, more substantial. It almost seemed as if the room was built to showcase Stephen's body, and the late afternoon light was allowed to shine only on Stephen. I couldn't take my eyes away from him, and when I did, I noticed that Nathan was staring at him too.

Nathan stepped forward to take the groceries and bring them into the kitchen. I walked closer to Stephen, unsure how to behave—as a friend or as a lover. He leaned down and gave me a chaste kiss on the cheek, which didn't clarify the situation. His skin smelled of salt, sun, and sea air. I envied his robust health and wished he could transfuse a small amount of his excess vitality into me.

"Where should I park my things?" he asked quietly.

I had been dreading this question. In my bedroom or with Nathan in the guest room? "Where would you be more comfortable?"

Stephen chuckled. "Oh! Very evasive!"

"Years of practice."

"Well, what do you think your son would prefer? If you have no preferences yourself…"

"I didn't say that," I replied, laughing.

"Not helpful, Bess! But as for Nathan?"

"I don't know. Why don't you place your suitcases in my room for now, and we'll see how the evening goes."

Stephen smiled and disappeared outside to get his luggage. I joined Nathan in the kitchen, where he was emptying the grocery bag. He set a potato with the others on the window sill, handed me a packet of steak, and withdrew a newspaper. After sitting at the table, he unfolded it to the first page.

I removed the other steaks from the refrigerator and began preparing a rub with various peppers and salt. After a few minutes, I asked Nathan if there was any news.

"Mmm. The authorities found the body of a seventy-one-year-old woman yesterday on the National Seashore. It says she drowned in the ocean at Head of the Meadow Beach two days ago, possibly caught in a rip current, though no rip currents were reported."

I turned to face Nathan. "Really? That's frightening. I was swimming near there yesterday. In fact, that's where I met Stephen."

I placed the steaks in a plastic bag, returned them to the refrigerator, and removed the zucchini and eggplant that Stephen had purchased earlier. On the chopping block, I sliced the vegetables lengthwise, adding olive oil and salt and pepper to both sides. Stephen entered the kitchen as Nathan turned to the second page and continued to read.

"The woman had a serious heart condition, so perhaps she had a heart attack and then drowned—that's what the police cite as an alternative reason for her death. They're doing an autopsy and an investigation."

Stephen looked over Nathan's shoulder at the newspaper. "Someone drowned?"

Nathan reprised part of the story.

"Well, most likely they'll find water in her lungs, which won't determine whether she died accidentally or deliberately," Stephen remarked. "The ocean was a little rough that day. Not like yesterday, which was calmer."

"So you were there when she was?" Nathan asked.

Stephen gazed at the small photo of the woman in the paper. "Yeah, I might have been, but I don't remember seeing her." He straightened and shook his head sadly. "Poor woman. Maybe her death was a blessing. I mean, if her heart was failing."

Nathan glanced at me over the edge of newspaper. "Do you think she killed herself?"

His question seemed loaded. Did he want to know if I'd considered such an option? As lightly as I could, I said I doubted it. One of those inane responses based on no information, but it seemed to appease him. He returned his attention to the newspaper, flipped the page, and kept reading.

"Bess, can I help?" Stephen asked.

"Could you scrub the potatoes, puncture them, and wrap each in aluminum foil? That's all we need to do at the moment," I replied. "And, if it's okay with you two gentlemen, I'm going to take a short nap before dinner. I run out of steam about this time each day."

No one objected, so I walked to the bedroom carrying my cell phone in case I felt like calling my friend Susan. Stephen's suitcase and beach gear were discreetly placed in the corner and several shirts and trousers were hung in the closet, pushed tightly together to take the minimum space. I liked the way he was cognizant of others. One of his many attributes.

As I laid down on the bed, I wondered what would happen tonight, whether we would abide by my decision not to have sex. Sleeping with Stephen, without making love, would seem strange, even if we weren't longstanding lovers. I thought of the night and morning we had shared and felt a sudden flush of desire, remembering how effortlessly he'd brought me to the peak of sensation, how tenderly and perfectly he'd touched me, as if he knew my body and what it needed. Our lovemaking had been otherworldly in its physical perfection, unlike any other sexual experience I'd ever had. Could I abstain once the bedroom door was closed? Or would attraction overpower my pain? Perhaps it would be prudent to ask Stephen to sleep in the room with Nathan, but that was awkward because I had no idea what Nathan thought of Stephen or what Stephen thought about my son.

I was too tired to mediate my warring impulses. Drifting off to sleep, I heard the men's voices and some footsteps—Nathan's—I knew his heavy tread well. Then the guest room door closed.

—

When I awoke from my nap, the room seemed unfamiliar until I remembered where I was and that I'd doubled the dose of fentanyl, probably causing my haziness. Most likely, I would adjust to the addition as I had to the single patch, but regardless of the increase, my back still hurt. I waited a few minutes for my mind to clear and then decided to call Susan. I reached for my phone and noted that Hugh had left two more messages, which I listened to—nothing new. "Where are you? When are you returning home?" and a belated expression of concern for my health at the end of the second message. Nathan, when he called before his arrival, had stated that he was coming to Provincetown. He didn't ask if it was okay or give an exact date. Susan's call was a standard "How are you?"

As I punched in her preset number, I pictured my friend. Susan Collier's shaggy dark brown hair had turned gray over the years so that she now resembled her dog, Finnegan, an Irish wolfhound, who weighed almost as much as Susan did. Susan had the brightest smile, one that always felt welcoming. Since our twenties, she had been my favorite companion, becoming even closer after my pancreatic cancer diagnosis. For a long time, Hugh and I had socialized with Susan and her husband, Lewis, a small, compact man. Pleasant and smart, he made a decent sidekick for Hugh, providing sufficient silence for Hugh to fill with conversation; Lewis being a man of few words and Hugh being a man of many. The two played golf and bridge on occasion, whereas Susan and I aimed for New York City to attend foreign films, concerts, and operas at the Met. At my behest and because of her natural diplomacy, Susan was civil to Hugh, though she disapproved of his callous behavior toward me, but during the last two years, we had agreed to avoid couples' evenings in favor of one-on-one outings.

Susan answered on the third ring.

"Oh, thank goodness! I was becoming worried, Bess!"

"Hi, sorry."

Susan didn't know precisely where I was, just that I'd left by car for the Cape. She had expressed apprehension about the risk; in fact, she had tried to dissuade me from making the trip.

"I've been sort of busy," I told her. "Nathan showed up unexpectedly."

I could hear relief in her voice. "That's great! I'm glad he's with you."

I explained about Nathan's layoff at work, then announced that I was filing for a divorce from Hugh. Several weeks ago, Susan had listened while I debated the issue and had put forth logistical reservations. In the end, she fully supported me if I decided to end the marriage.

"Well, it will be a challenge," Susan warned.

"I know, but Nathan just said he's coming to live at home for a while. To help."

"Oh, my! You must be so pleased! That will be important for both of you. And as for Hugh, the hell with him."

I laughed at Susan's exuberance, which was one aspect of her personality I treasured. "Well, we'll see how it goes with Hugh."

"You know, I must have been thinking something was about to happen because this morning I suddenly remembered that night several months after you started chemo. When you and Hugh invited us for dinner."

"Oh, dear. I recall that infamous evening very clearly."

"We had some wine, and after we ate, you felt sick and went to bed," Susan recounted. "And then your dear husband had the gall to mention how attractive the new young administrator was, the woman he'd been flirting with at the departmental party. The party you were too ill to attend."

"You were pretty mad. I could hear you shouting at him from upstairs."

"He deserved it, the jerk. For that and for all the other times." She chuckled. "Poor Lewis was practically hiding under the table. I don't get angry often, but when I do..." She paused and laughed again. "Anyway, Bess, you're doing the right thing."

"Thanks, Susan. By the way, please don't tell Hugh or Lewis about the divorce papers arriving."

"No, I won't. Besides, I'm in Chicago with my mother so I won't be in Stamford until two days before school starts. Mom fell and fractured her arm. She's decided to move in with us, so I'm packing her things."

"Oh, what a shame! Is she okay?"

"She's in a cast and is a little sore from taking a tumble. Otherwise, she's fine."

"Let's hope the break heals fast," I replied. "I imagine this must feel like a mixed blessing. You've been trying to convince her to come to Stamford for several years."

"I know but I'm glad that Mom realizes she can't manage on her own."

"Will you please give her my love?"

"I will, Bess. Now, I hate to dash, but I have to take a chicken out of the oven. We'll get together as soon as I return to Stamford."

"Sounds great." I wished her a safe trip and ended the call, though I wanted to talk with Susan longer, to tell her about the physical changes I was experiencing, and to confide about Stephen, though I felt some reluctance about admitting to my infidelity. Of course, Susan would dismiss my guilt as laughable in light of Hugh's transgressions. When I saw her, I would decide whether to reveal what happened. By then, the affair would probably be just a fading memory. Stephen would return to Boston, and I'd probably never hear from him again.

I glanced at my watch and saw that it was almost 6:30. As I rose from the bed, I heard Nathan leave the guest room and Stephen's voice in the hall or living room. After I cleaned my face, I walked to the kitchen. Stephen was arranging a plate of appetizers, and Nathan had already opened a bottle of red wine and was well into his first glass. For a fleeting moment, I thought of them as "boys" because Nathan still seemed like one, and Stephen might be closer in age to my son than he was to me, though I had no idea how old he was. None of the details of his biography had shed any light on that. On reflection, I knew surprisingly little about him. Perhaps during the evening I would learn more.

Stephen poured me some wine, and we ventured outdoors. Nathan and I sat at the table while Stephen dumped charcoal into the grill, lit the briquettes, and stood back to admire the sudden flames that burst upward. I observed how the yellow, orange, and red fingers of fire reflected in his pale blue eyes and danced across the taut planes of his face. It was as if he had transformed into the god Vulcan or perhaps Hades, god of the underworld, emerging from the fiery pit of the grill. I mused on my likening of Stephen to a god, but the comparison was fair. From Nathan's rapt expression as he watched Stephen, my son was probably entertaining similar thoughts.

Stephen settled in the chair across from me. The angled golden light from the sun replaced the magical illumination from the flames, tinting his white hair so that it appeared almost blond. He gave me a cheerful smile and lifted his glass in a silent toast. I acknowledged him and took a sip. My intention was to drink moderately tonight, which was aided by the choice of California merlot brought by Nathan. I preferred dry whites, a fact he had probably forgotten.

"So, Stephen, you said you live in Boston. Where did you grow up?" Nathan asked.

"I moved around a lot when I was young. Connecticut, Long Island, and Rhode Island."

"Was your father in the military?"

"No."

"All those places are near water," I commented.

Stephen laughed and looked away, as if disinclined to talk about himself. "Yeah, always near water."

"Parents? Brothers and sisters?" Nathan persisted.

Stephen turned his focus on Nathan. For a second, Stephen's

expression stiffened. Then, recovering his smile and his pleasant manner, he said, "I'm an orphan."

The admission dropped like a hand grenade into the conversation. Both Nathan and I fell silent. While Stephen had mentioned this in a matter-of-fact manner, the comment seemed terse and almost jarring. Why hadn't he divulged this significant fact when he and I were trading our histories? The omission seemed odd, perhaps deliberate, although I hadn't talked about my parents much, either, except to say my father died from cancer.

"I'm sorry to hear that, Stephen," I replied. "Were you adopted at birth or as a baby?"

"My mother left before I was two, though I don't remember her or the separation. After that, I was sent to a nice couple in East Hampton and stayed with them for five years. But when they were killed in a boating accident, I was returned to the orphanage."

"A boating accident? Were you with them?" I asked.

Stephen nodded. "I jumped overboard a second before the crash."

How many children that age would jump from a moving boat? That sounded peculiar. His description of early dislocation also sent off my therapist's alarm. Trauma to infants before the age of two often produced serious psychological effects, and whatever damage he'd experienced might have been compounded by the second loss of his first adopted family.

"What made you do that? Jump?"

"I don't know why I did. A little precognition?" He shrugged. "It was low tide and the outboard hit a submerged rock. We weren't far from shore."

"So you weren't hurt and were able to swim to safety?"

"Yes. Luckily I've always been at home in the water."

"Oh, Stephen, that must have been frightening! You were very young."

He sighed. "It wasn't easy."

When Stephen said "it wasn't easy," I recalled his earlier use of the phrase, in reference to his life. Was this some kind of euphemism that meant the opposite? Certainly his youth hadn't been a "happy cruise," either. If anyone knew Stephen well, such as Terry's closest friends, those they shared in common, wouldn't they be aware of his tragic losses and be more sympathetic after Terry died rather than behave as Stephen had described?

"I'm sure it wasn't easy." I examined his face and saw little evidence that the discussion pained him, only that he was disinclined to talk about it. "Did another family adopt you?"

He reached for his wine, took a swallow, and replaced the glass on the placemat. "Yeah. Pretty soon afterward, another couple took me in. I liked them a lot. Their house was small, but it was near the water, in Connecticut. We did a lot of sailing."

Did orphanages place children in such diverse locations? Perhaps it was possible. "What happened then?" As I asked this, I sensed that another misfortune would be revealed.

Stephen sighed again. "Well, a year later, when I was eight, my adopted mother had a stroke and died a few weeks afterward. My father was in shock because her death was so unexpected. Taking care of me proved too much for him, especially since he traveled a lot for work, so I was sent back." He leaned against his chair, as if he wished to physically distance himself from the conversation. "After that, I stayed with several families on a trial basis. Some were nice, some weren't, but nothing worked out. I lived in foster houses until I came of age."

From all I knew about childhood development and from dealing with three clients with similar histories—though none as terrible as Stephen's—having multiple failed adoptions usually indicated that the child suffered from significant emotional problems. These disorders could be exacerbated by the all-too-common placement in abusive homes or orphanages. However, despite Stephen's painful history, I hadn't detected any disturbed behavior or instability. Quite the opposite. He appeared very well adjusted, agreeable, socially adept, and empathetic—one of the qualities first to be jettisoned in troubled children. How could Stephen survive these repetitive losses without being seriously scarred? How could anyone?

I didn't know what to say, but I reminded myself that I'd been in this speechless state thousands of times during my practice. I exhaled slowly, trying to relax. "I can't believe all that occurred to you, Stephen. All those homes and different families…the deaths."

"Just bad luck. Especially for my first two sets of parents."

His calm acceptance further surprised me. Although Stephen exhibited some resignation as he spoke, there were no traces of deep residual injury, of devastation or resentment at the unfair life he had experienced. I thought about his relationship with Terry, which sounded like the only committed connection he'd ever established, though Stephen said it had lasted about a year. Considering the many rejections and abandonments he'd just recounted, Terry's death should have sent Stephen spinning with grief—more so than for most people. Yet, on balance, his reaction to the loss seemed sorrowful but more or less appropriate.

During our conversation, Nathan hadn't participated, though he had been drinking steadily. After eating a piece of cheese, he said, "Do you know who your real parents are?"

Stephen turned toward Nathan. "I did but I've lost track of them. They were older so they're probably gone by now." He smiled again, as if the circumstances of his childhood no longer mattered.

They wouldn't be that old, but I wasn't certain of Stephen's age. His offhand dismissal amplified the strangeness. Most orphans I'd seen in therapy were intensely curious about their birth parents and usually were either hurt or angry about their abandonment. Sometimes they wanted to reconnect with them, to understand the reasons for their rejection and to learn about their ancestry, whether they had siblings or other relatives. Stephen displayed none of these emotions, nor did he seem particularly interested in his family origins. In fact, he had been sitting quietly, with his hands resting on the table.

Then he broke from his immobility, crossed his legs and focused on Nathan. "Hey, how about you, Nathan? Did you grow up in Stamford?"

Nathan gaped for a second, obviously still absorbing Stephen's story and disconcerted by the sudden change in the conversation. Finally, he nodded. "Yeah, I did, but after university in California, I moved to Manhattan. I've lived there for the last twelve years."

"Hmm. Maybe that's where I've seen you before. In the city."

Nathan unfurled his shirt's long sleeve, refolded it to the same length, just below his elbow, and shrugged. "No, I'm sure we haven't met."

"Hmm. Could have sworn we did. Somewhere. Well, perhaps you're right." Stephen nodded his head slightly, a small tell that contradicted his agreement with Nathan. This led me to wonder if my son had encountered Stephen, though it seemed unlikely.

Nathan's gaze migrated to the dunes behind us, where the sun was casting dark shadows under the trees. He was biting his lip.

11

~~~~~

Stephen asked Nathan about his father, perhaps to hear a second perspective other than mine or to draw Nathan into the conversation, away from a discussion of Stephen's own history.

Nathan fortified himself with wine before answering. "My father is a cheating bastard." He delivered this statement without amplification and seemed content with its blunt accuracy, as if he was matching Stephen's terse comment about being an orphan but doing so with bitterness.

Stephen looked as startled by the unflinching pronouncement as I was. Although I was tempted to rebut Nathan's sour remark, I didn't trust myself to make a temperate response.

"Really?" Stephen said at last.

"Really." Nathan leaned forward. "He's been cheating on my mother since I was a little kid. Of course, I wasn't aware of what was going on until later. I wouldn't be surprised if he's sleeping with some gal half his age right now."

The declarative tone in Nathan's voice was unmistakable. Was he really angry at Hugh or was he obliquely challenging Stephen—calling him out for spending the night with me? Or was he criticizing me for not leaving Hugh sooner?

"What's upsetting you, Nathan?" I asked. "You're being very disrespectful of your father." When he didn't answer, I said, "Yes, you're right. Hugh has had affairs, and, yes, they hurt me and they hurt you. I should have divorced him long ago. I wish I had and I'm sorry I didn't. But your father loves you. He would be devastated to hear you talking about him like this."

He took another gulp of wine. "Well, maybe he needs to be devastated."

I was surprised by my son's heated reaction. "Regardless of how you feel, this isn't the time or place to attack Hugh."

"You mean not in front of Stephen? You don't want him to know our family secrets?"

I glanced at Stephen, who appeared uncomfortable. "That's not the point. It's not fair to criticize Hugh when he can't defend himself," I replied. "If you have a problem with your father, deal with him directly."

"You've always covered for him," Nathan retorted. "I don't get it. I never have."

"Marriages are complicated."

He flipped his hand in the air, as if to dismiss my comment. "Ha! That's an easy out!"

"No, it's a true statement. You need to look at both sides of a relationship to understand how it works."

"I *am* looking at both sides." He stared hard at me. "Remember? I was there. In the middle. For all those years."

I exhaled slowly, trying to diffuse my irritation. "What are you saying, Nathan? That you're mad at me?"

He jerked his head, as if taken aback by my directness, and then gave Stephen a sidelong look to gauge his reaction. Stephen met his gaze, but his expression remained impassive, which seemed to cool my son's antagonism. Nathan slowly relaxed, though traces of irritation ruffled the set of his mouth. "Never mind, Mom. We're fine."

I wasn't sure if Nathan was being sarcastic or honest or what had caused his prickly mood. Had it begun with Stephen's suggestion that they might have met before? "Okay. If that changes, let's talk about it."

Everyone became quiet. Stephen broke up the tense silence

by standing to add potatoes to the bottom of the grill. "An hour before dinner," he announced, replacing the domed top.

We needed to switch to a less provocative topic, so I related my conversation with Susan, explaining that her mother was coming to live with Susan and Lewis and why.

"Her mother's getting pretty old, isn't she?" Nathan asked.

"Eighty-eight."

Stephen returned to the table. "It's a difficult decision for someone that age to make. Giving up their home and living with an adult child."

Nathan and I exchanged glances. He was the adult child who was returning to live with me, and I was the one who might be giving up my autonomy. What I'd imagined as a safe subject was proving to have thorns.

"Yes, it is," I agreed.

"So that means Mrs. Collier won't be available often, right?" Nathan asked.

Was he pleased that Susan would be busy? It sounded that way. "I'm sure she'll be around." I certainly hoped so. I also hoped that Nathan wasn't developing a territorial attitude about my care.

—

The conversation branched into new subjects. I watched the two men interact, which they were now doing in a friendlier fashion. Nathan's demeanor had migrated into careful reserve, but he inserted a few spiky observations that were annoying. Was he testing Stephen's patience or mine? Whatever his intent, Stephen managed Nathan with equanimity, while I kept my hands on the arms of the chair in an attempt to appear composed, a pose Stephen mirrored. In fact, as I sifted through various mental snapshots from our time together, it occurred to me that Stephen rarely exhibited emotion through movement; instead, he usually sat still. Very unlike my son, whose feelings were signaled through gestures, fidgets, and the language of his body rather than through verbal communication. When Nathan did speak, he often had difficulty moderating his remarks, as he had this evening.

Since they had become a couple, I'd noticed Melissa often tried to smooth over Nathan's occasional rough-edged manner much as I always had. Her ability to do this gracefully was one reason I liked Melissa and possibly one reason he had been attracted to her—because she reminded him of me. The Imago model posits that people tend to enter relationships with partners who are like one of their parents, because of similar good or bad traits or both. As for the cause of their break up, had Melissa grown weary of tamping down Nathan's hot spots? Or had Nathan resented Melissa's mild corrections?

I came to my feet. "Nathan, dear, would you mind helping me in the kitchen for a minute?"

Nathan drained his glass. "Sure. Need to open another bottle anyway."

He stood, and as Stephen started to do the same, I extended my hand to indicate that he should stay outside. "We'll be right back."

—

I laced my arm through my son's as we entered the kitchen.

"What do you want me to do?" he asked.

I steered him into the living room where our conversation couldn't be overheard. "Nathan, something is bothering you."

He shrugged and looked away from me. "No, there isn't. I'm fine."

The general approach wouldn't work. A process of elimination was required. "Did I say or do anything that distressed you?"

"No."

With my fingers, I moved his chin so that he was forced to face me. "Are you worried about Melissa and your job?"

"Yeah, but we've talked about that."

We had but I still didn't know details about what happened with Melissa. Was the issue with her connected to whatever troubled him now?

"Okay, well, that leaves Stephen. While I was taking a nap, did you two have a disagreement?"

"No." He thrust his hands in his pockets, trying to appear unconcerned, but the gesture came across as defensive.

"Are you disturbed about him?"

He shrugged again.

We were going in circles and not landing anywhere. "Nathan, please help me. I can see that you're not yourself."

"Well, all right." He sighed impatiently. "I'm not happy he's here. I expected to be alone with you. To be there for you. And, instead, you're with this guy who looks like...a damned super model."

"To begin, I had no idea you were coming—"

"I emailed and left phone messages," he protested, his balance shifting, unsettled by alcohol. He spread his feet apart to steady himself.

"None of which I read or heard, Nathan. I'm sorry. My whole idea of getting away was to be disconnected for a few days to think."

"You didn't stay disconnected long."

I couldn't hide my irritation. "That's not very fair, and it's not very nice."

"Maybe it isn't, but I can't stand the idea of the two of you in bed together." He scrunched up his eyes, as if by doing so he could blot out the image.

"It's not easy for me to imagine you making love to Melissa, either," I replied in a measured voice. "That's the way it is with parents and children. We don't like to think our mothers and fathers or sons and daughters are sexual beings."

"Yeah, I guess," Nathan said without much conviction.

"I can't erase what occurred with Stephen, nor do I really want to do that. It was a simple, surprising connection that made me feel better about myself. That might seem superficial, but sometimes a brief encounter can lift one's outlook. To be honest, last night was one of the most extraordinary evenings I've experienced in the last several years. I felt very complimented by his interest. Considering my present state, that kind of evening is not going to happen again."

Nathan stared at his shoes and didn't speak for a moment. Finally, he apologized. "Sorry, Mom. I'm out of line." He hesitated and then added, "It's just that you came to get away, and I came to get away too. Away from work, Melissa, and my father. Instead, I'm faced with a guy who makes me feel like a total loser. He's everything I'm not. Dad would love him."

I placed my hand on his cheek. "Oh, Nathan, that's not true! You're not a loser! You know that. This is a bad time, a very bad time, but it won't last forever. And, yes, Stephen is really handsome, but he's hurting. His life is in turmoil like yours is."

Nathan encircled my shoulders, swaying slightly. Perhaps realizing he was unsteady, he disengaged and stood there, his forehead furrowed and his eyes downcast. "Yeah, I know, Mom. But I feel like he's taking you away from me."

"Oh, Nathan! He isn't. Not in the least. And he won't. You can't imagine how moved I am that you came to Provincetown. It means everything that you did, dear. You're the most important person in the world to me. You always have been." I gave his arm a small squeeze to emphasize my point. "I understand all this is confusing. I'm not settled about the situation with Stephen myself."

His eyes raised, and, as I had done so often over the years, I reached up and smoothed his hair. "Nathan, would you prefer that Stephen slept in the guest room tonight? With you?"

He regarded me with a conflicted expression. "No, Mom. You do whatever you want to do. I'll work it out."

"Are you sure?"

Nathan nodded.

I kissed him quickly, hoping peace was restored between us, yet not absolutely convinced that it was. Nor was I absolutely convinced that his jealousy of Susan and Stephen had been erased. In fact, it occurred to me that with Hugh out of the house, Nathan might be seeking to establish a primary position in my life.

Although I'm not a Freudian analyst, I wondered if this was some kind of buried Oedipal wish that was being exposed.

We returned to the kitchen. While Nathan uncorked a bottle of white wine, I removed the vegetables and steaks from the refrigerator, and then we carried everything outside. Stephen was leaning back in his chair, staring upward. A few silver stars were tentatively piercing the clear blue sky. If I made a wish, would it be for a long life and the disappearance of cancer? No. I would wish for Nathan to be happy, to create a place for himself that included a woman who loved him and work that held meaning.

When we approached, Stephen lowered his gaze from the heavens and straightened in his chair. A slight frown formed as he stared at both of us.

"Everything okay?" he asked.

"Yeah," Nathan replied, filling Stephen's glass. "We're switching to white wine because of Mom. Hope you don't mind?"

"Not as long as it has alcohol in it!"

———

Dinner went without further disruption. The steaks were perfectly cooked, as were the slices of zucchini and eggplant. Unfortunately, my chronic issue with constipation made me feel full and queasy. This was a treacherous side effect of the opiate drugs, one I'd wrestled with for months. My digestive system was often wrenched in knots, requiring a lot of time in the bathroom and fussing with laxatives, fiber pills, and various natural food remedies, none of which were consistently successful. I apologized for my lack of appetite and hinted at the cause but didn't belabor the subject. Nathan would learn soon enough about all the gritty physical problems I contended with on a daily basis.

Stephen smiled in commiseration. He probably understood how I felt, assuming Terry had dealt with similar difficulties. Either that or he was aware of the common adverse reaction to extended use of painkillers.

"Shall we share the rest of Bess' steak?" Nathan asked Stephen.

While they ate the meat, half of my potato, and finished the bottle of wine, I observed the two men, but mostly my son. It had been a long while since I'd had an opportunity to see him interact without the presence of Melissa and, more notably, without Hugh, who usually tilted the conversation toward himself and away from Nathan, unless he was falsely flattering him—which Nathan saw through immediately—or he was instructing Nathan how to better his life, one form of unintentional disparagement. Between the recent events with Melissa and the job loss, I realized my son wasn't coping well. Add in the stress of my illness and he was in deeper water. It had always been my role to rescue him, doing so in an indirect manner. Now I regretted that I might have helped him too much, too often, and that Nathan might not possess the necessary fight to save himself. Could he resurrect his sense of worth? Take justifiable pride in his many real accomplishments? Hold his head up, regroup, and march forward? And could he do this without Melissa and without me?

Nathan needed to be strong, so that when I relinquished myself to death, he would survive and find happiness. But watching his petulance, irritability, and possessiveness, I concluded that my son was much weaker and more anxious than I had assumed, an awareness that filled me with overwhelming sadness. What could I do to steady his future course in the time I had left? Somehow, it was critical that I find a way to model independence and fortitude. Yet the reverse was also true. I needed to show Nathan how to let others take charge, to accept their love and care with grateful appreciation, a lesson I was slowly learning.

Nathan and Stephen seemed to be getting along, though my son was continuing to drink a lot, another issue of concern. Stephen was holding his own in terms of sobriety, but he outweighed Nathan by thirty pounds and tolerated liquor better, almost as if it didn't affect him at all. In fact, I remembered that last night, despite imbibing nearly two bottles of wine, Stephen had appeared quite sober during our conversation and lovemaking.

Nathan chewed his last bite of steak, swallowed, and laid the knife and fork on his plate. "Hey, how about some of the pinot grigio I brought?"

I didn't want any, but he had already bolted from the table. I looked at Stephen, who made no comment except to glance at Nathan's empty glass and shake his head slightly.

After Nathan returned, he started to pour more wine for Stephen.

"I'll wait a bit," Stephen said.

"Me, too," I agreed.

Nathan shrugged. "Okay. Whatever." He filled his glass and, while standing, took a long drink. Then he regained his chair, leaned forward, and rested his elbow on the table. His pose was nonchalant, or trying to appear so, yet he kept rubbing his fingers together like they were dry sticks that might produce a fire.

Addressing Stephen, Nathan asked, "So, you're gay?"

12

At first, I thought his question was straightforward, a simple conversational gambit, but Nathan's expression had darkened.

Stephen smiled and laced his fingers behind his head. "I was just in a committed gay relationship, which you know, right?"

"So does that make you homosexual? Or what?"

Stephen chuckled. "It doesn't make me anything. I'm not fond of labels."

I was stunned by Nathan's exhibition of overt prejudice, for that's what his barbed tone implied. Only once had I witnessed this kind of behavior from my son—when my colleague David came to the house with his partner, Paul. Nathan, a teenager, had refused to sit at the dining table with the two men. His rudeness had disturbed Hugh and myself, and, after David and Paul left, Hugh confronted Nathan upstairs in his room. I didn't hear what transpired, but I'd never seen any anti-gay prejudice since, though David didn't visit again and eventually moved to another psychotherapy practice. Remembering this hostile behavior, I decided to intervene. Before I could, Nathan continued.

"I love labels. I'm a heterosexual," he said, almost grimly, as he fussed at a bit of food on the placemat. "Are you? I mean, you just slept with my mother."

"Nathan, what's the matter?" I asked.

Nathan flicked at the crumb and sent it spinning across the

table. "The matter? I can't figure out why Stephen—this paragon of good looks—would go for you."

This insult stung. How could my son say this, especially after I'd just told him how complimented I was by Stephen's attention? I felt my face heat with embarrassment and anger.

Stephen unfolded his hands and laid them on the table. "Why wouldn't I be attracted to Bess? She's intelligent, kind, and beautiful. I'm fortunate to have met her."

Nathan's eyes smoldered and his grip tightened around his wine glass. "Because you can pick up any hot guy in town. All you'd have to do is snap your fingers."

"Hey! Maybe you need to chill out." Stephen kept his face composed, but I could tell he was annoyed.

Nathan wiped his mouth briskly with his napkin. "Why should I? I want to know your angle. What you're after."

"Nathan, that's enough," I said, with a force I seldom used. "I don't understand why you're being so impolite. Please apologize to Stephen."

"I will if he promises not to have sex with you again."

I felt my own hands tighten and saw that Stephen's lips were set in a taut line. I wanted to demand that Nathan go to his room, to treat him like an out-of-control child. "Where is all this coming from?" I asked. "This isn't about Stephen, so why pretend that it is? It's either about me or about something else that's been triggered by him."

Nathan glanced in my direction, a look that communicated two conflicting emotions vying for supremacy. Belligerence won out. He added more wine into his glass.

"Like I said, I want him to promise."

"What happens between us is our business," I replied. "Earlier, I asked if you wanted Stephen to sleep in the guest room rather than with me. You said no. That I should do as I wished. Well, live with that, Nathan, and stop this attack on Stephen. It's not warranted and it's very unbecoming. You were not raised this way."

"No, I was raised to be a raving adulterer by dear old dad," he retorted, taking a large swallow from his glass. "Great role model."

"Bess, if you want me to leave, I will," Stephen interjected.

"No, Stephen. Thank you." I looked at my son and noted the stubborn set of his jaw. "Perhaps you should take a long walk and settle down."

Nathan snorted, made no comment, and finished his wine. "Okay, maybe I will."

He lurched unsteadily to his feet, bumped the table with his hip, and walked into the house. The screen door slammed behind him, either intentionally or due to drunkenness. I turned to watch Nathan in the kitchen. He was struggling with the corkscrew, attempting to open the fourth bottle. When he was successful, he grabbed the bottle and exited through the living room.

"I apologize, Stephen," I began. "I don't know what's wrong with him."

"I hope I'm not the cause. I'd hate to think he's troubling you because of me."

I considered possible explanations. "It's almost like he's pushing us together by this insane attack, by insulting both of us." I shook my head. "Or he's trying to justify the anger he feels, though I don't know what the source of his anger is. And now he's got another bottle of wine. Heaven knows what effect that will have."

Stephen came to his feet and began stacking the plates. "I was serious about returning to the motel. I don't want you to feel divided between us."

I rose and grabbed silverware and napkins. "If you left, that would condone Nathan's conduct. Not to mention I don't want you to leave. Let's do the dishes and go to bed. If he comes back and continues, I'll speak to him."

"Whatever you want, Bess."

—

In the bedroom, Stephen opened the windows for some fresh air and changed into striped drawstring pants topped by a bright white tee shirt. As I pulled on my blue pajamas, I dithered about whether to lock the bedroom door and decided that doing so might infuriate Nathan more if he tried the knob. But I was almost equally concerned that he would barge in, drunk and hostile, and find us asleep or otherwise engaged. Although my son wasn't physically abusive and I wasn't concerned for our safety, he was acting so oddly that I had no idea what to expect.

As tired as I was, I felt edgy and tense. I considered taking a sleeping pill, but I never mixed sleeping medication with wine, even though I had drunk less than two glasses.

"Come on, Bess. You look exhausted."

Stephen led me to the bed, slipped in beside me, placed his arm around my shoulders, and drew me close against him. My cheek rested on his firm, rounded chest, against the soft cotton of his shirt, and though I still wondered why he desired this intimacy, I was grateful for the comfort he provided. I wanted to close my eyes and sleep, protected in his embrace, savoring this unique communion with a caring man, yet Nathan's demand to know what Stephen wanted was ringing in my ears. Was Stephen seeking some kind of mother figure? A substitute for the woman who had deserted him at birth and for those adopted mothers who had died? I saw no evidence to support this possibility, but the thought added to my confusion.

I tipped my head to look into Stephen's blue eyes. Tonight, they appeared darker due to the low light emanating from the single bedside lamp. "Stephen, how can I ask this?"

"Ask what?"

"Will you forgive me for wondering why you're here, with me? I'm sure your reasons are sincere but—"

"Nathan has created doubts?"

"Yes."

He smiled. "Well, I could be anywhere, but for now, this is where I want to be. There's some quality in you, Bess, that makes me feel calm. Maybe it's your melodic voice that I find relaxing. I can't explain it."

"Even with all of Nathan's unpleasantness?"

"Yeah. And I wouldn't worry about Nathan. I think he'll figure out what's disturbing him. Some realizations are close to breaking through. That's my guess."

"Hmm. Do you think so?"

Stephen nodded.

"I'm glad to hear that because his behavior has been a huge shock." I paused to consider the optimism embedded in Stephen's remark. It was astonishing that I, his mother, who knew Nathan so well, had formed the opposite opinion, a pessimistic one. "I know I should trust that my son will be fine—"

"Afterward?"

"Yes." I swallowed hard. "Ever since my diagnosis, I've been worried about what will happen to him after I die. Seeing how he's just acted, hearing what he said, well, I'm scared he won't manage alone." I shook my head. "How I wish I could share your belief in him!"

"He'll be okay. I'm certain of it," Stephen replied. "And, as for tonight, perhaps he'll pass out from the wine and wake to an amazing epiphany. I wouldn't be surprised if that happened."

"What a relief that would be! It's so challenging to be a parent. Fretting about children and blaming yourself when they have difficulties, even if their problems have little to do with you."

"I can imagine." Stephen hugged me. "Let's see how he does. Think positive thoughts."

"I will. And the good news is that Nathan plans to come home for a while. At least until he finds another job."

Stephen smiled. "Oh. He does? I'm sure you're very happy about that."

"I am. He'll be a big help, especially without Hugh around."

We said no more about my son. I asked Stephen about his first adopted parents, but he suggested we talk more when I wasn't so tired. As much as I wanted to express my concern and to learn details about his experience, he was correct. I was totally spent. The warmth of his body and my weariness blended together, making me drowsy. He turned out the light, and we lay in the darkness, holding each other. I felt his serenity flow into me like liquid anesthesia. While Stephen and I didn't love each other in a traditional way, love of a kind flowed between us, a buoyant current that carried us along without aiming at a goal or destination. Objectives—other than those of a practical sort—had ceased to matter to me and seemed inconsequential to him. Therefore, from my perspective, Nathan's insistence that Stephen wanted something from our relationship felt incongruent and didn't fit Stephen's selfless attitude.

As I considered this handsome man, I wondered what forces had brought us together and for what purpose. I didn't believed in fate, but Stephen's arrival in my life seemed auspicious, as was, perhaps, my entrance into his. Gratitude swept over me and I succumbed to sleep.

—

I woke when the door to the bedroom opened. A bright triangle of light pierced the blackness and struck my face. In the center of the light, my son stood, his silhouetted form still and dark. I jumped as did Stephen. We both stared at Nathan for a few seconds, then Stephen separated from me, swung his legs to the side of the bed, and was about to turn on the lamp when Nathan spoke.

"No lights," he said in a loud whisper.

I started to tell Nathan to go to sleep, but Stephen leaned over and grasped my arm, as if to silence me.

"Stephen?" Nathan's voice inflected like he was asking a question, but the effect came across as a summons or a plea.

I had no idea what was the matter and teetered between alarm and curiosity as Stephen stood, crossed the room, and dwarfed the rectangular space of the open door, blocking my son from sight. Slowly, Stephen stepped across the threshold and closed the door behind him.

I lay against the pillows, my heart racing from the sudden awakening. The image of Nathan was etched in my mind like some kind of eerie, high-contrast, black-and-white photograph. In the darkness, my eyes reversed the impression, making the opening black and his figure white, and then the two reversed to reality once again. Was this a symbolic depiction of my son's mystifying behavior this evening, his Jekyll-and-Hyde impersonation? Did Nathan's request to Stephen mean he wanted to make peace or was he still angry and wanted to have an argument? Because I didn't know, I felt a measure of dread that something combustible would occur, exacerbated by Nathan's heavy drinking. I hoped my anxieties were baseless and that Stephen would impart some wise words to my son or that the epiphany Stephen had predicted would occur.

I waited, unsure whether I should join them in the living room. Yet Nathan had asked for Stephen, not me.

—

Their conversation outside my room was unintelligible. Soon, I couldn't hear the men at all, perhaps because they had moved into the kitchen or outside on the patio. Tiredness overcame me, and I drifted off to sleep for a short time. When I woke, I heard no voices, laughter, or creaking floorboards. I tossed off the sheet and began to stand, then detected a noise in the guest room. Was Nathan going to bed? If so, where was Stephen? Had he chosen to sleep on the couch in order not to wake me? Or was he using the second twin bed for the same reason? I listened more intently. The wind was rising, sighing above the roof and around the cottage's snug girth. A pine branch outside my window scratched on the glass, and a distant owl was calling, its feathery voice shivering through the trees. These sounds left me feeling alone, a sensation that I hadn't experienced during my first night here when I had been by myself. The irony of coming to Truro for solitude, and then regretting having it, wasn't lost on me.

Although the bed felt empty, it was best to let Stephen sleep where he wished.

—

In the morning, when I opened my eyes, I felt confused, as if part of me was clinging to sleep, refusing to depart from a seductive dream about Stephen, a magnificent fantasy in which I almost believed he was alive, yet he was too ideal to be a living man. We had never met on the beach or participated in amazing sex. We hadn't shared our intimate thoughts and feelings. Although I felt incredibly sad that Stephen was imaginary, an illusion fueled by opiates and exhaustion, it made more sense than that he was mortal.

I let out a measured breath and felt the pain radiating through my chest and back. The discomfort, the room, the cottage, my trip to Truro were tangible and real. The rest was not.

And then I turned over. In the early morning light, I saw Stephen lying beside me, facing the far wall. I lurched backward, stunned, and stared at his thick white hair and massive shoulders, the pale skin on the nape of his neck. The air held the subtle scent of his cool, clean cologne. He did exist! Suddenly, I remembered last night, when he left the room to speak with Nathan. What had the two discussed? And, afterward, how had he reentered the room and laid on the bed without waking me? I'm a light sleeper, sensitive to noise or physical disturbance. Had Stephen simply materialized?

He felt me stir, rolled over, and smiled. "Good morning, Bess." In these few minutes, the sun seemed to have risen quickly, as if it had hurried to illuminate Stephen's face.

"Good morning," I whispered, still surprised by his presence. I tried to organize my chaotic thoughts and finally said, "Where did you go with Nathan last night? I didn't notice that you returned."

"I can be incredibly quiet. Glad I didn't bother you." Stephen kissed my cheek and placed his arm under my pillow. "Did you miss me?" he asked, with a devilish twinkle in his eyes.

"I did." He hadn't explained what happened with Nathan.

He laughed and pulled me close. "Well, I missed you too."

His hand pressed on my back and I winced.

"Does that hurt?" he asked, loosening his embrace.

I nodded and struggled to sit upright. "It does. I don't know what's going on."

Stephen was quiet, as if analyzing the level and location of the pain. "You seem worse, Bess."

I didn't want to admit this to him or to myself. "Maybe I'll feel better after breakfast."

This was nonsensical, and Stephen raised one eyebrow, as if to disagree, but didn't argue. "Well, okay. I bought cranberry scones yesterday at a bakery."

"Good. Thank you." The last thing I wanted was anything heavy to eat.

He kissed me again and we separated, rising from opposite sides of the bed.

"By the way, where is Nathan? I mean, where did he sleep?" I asked, pulling on my bathrobe.

Stephen leaned over to place his feet in his slippers. "In his room."

13

Before Stephen showered, he replaced the older fentanyl patch on my back but didn't comment on the double dose, though his hand lingered on my skin, perhaps sensing the heat emanating from the tumors. I took two ibuprofen, doubting their efficacy, donned my bathrobe, and walked into the kitchen. All the glasses were washed and replaced in the cabinets. The room was spotless, as if two guys hadn't been carousing into the wee hours of the night. Probably Stephen's doing because Nathan was famous for leaving a mess. The white filter was already perched in the Melitta's brown cone, the water was in the kettle, and three juice glasses and three sets of silverware were placed on the table. I was impressed.

When Stephen joined me, I thanked him. Then we heard Nathan bang into something in the guest room and curse.

Stephen said, "He's probably got a terrible hangover."

"I bet he does." I began boiling water while Stephen poured orange juice.

"I'm sure you're wondering what went on last night," Stephen began, as he took a seat at the table.

I turned to face him. "Yes, I am."

He rubbed his chin. "Well, like you, I respect confessions when asked, so I can't tell you a lot. I think that Nathan will feel better—except for a headache—and will act very differently today."

I let out a relieved sigh. "I hope so. Thank you for whatever you did. I greatly appreciate it."

He smiled. "Oh, I didn't do much."

I let it go and attended to the coffee.

—

When Nathan stumped into the kitchen, he looked awful. Red eyes, flushed complexion, head held low, either due to fatigue or embarrassment. He gave me a clumsy hug and apologized for making a scene and being ill-mannered the night before.

"It won't happen again," he promised, giving Stephen's shoulder a quick squeeze.

This sign of camaraderie was as much of a surprise as Nathan's changed demeanor. Had Stephen waved a magic wand over my son? I heated the scones, divided mine in half, and split one of the halves in two, placing the quarters on Stephen's and Nathan's plates. The constipation had worsened overnight, and the thought of eating made me feel ill, but I joined Stephen and Nathan at the table and admired how the morning sun was streaming through the windows. Judging by the warm breeze circulating around the room, the day would be hot. I asked if the two men were going to the beach.

Stephen and Nathan exchanged glances, leaving me to conclude they'd already discussed plans last night. Unless I was mistaken, the dynamics in our three-way relationship had altered. Yesterday, the bonds between my son and me had been strong, and the one between myself and Stephen had secondarily been close. Between Stephen and Nathan? Tentative. Now the triangle seemed more equilateral in nature.

Nathan laughed. "I'm not so sure I want to swim in shark-infested waters."

"Hey, don't worry. I'll protect you." Stephen chuckled and turned toward me. "Bess, are you going to come with us?"

The "us" in his comment and the teasing confirmed my suspicion that they had become friendlier. While I was glad if this was true, I was apprehensive about the sudden realignment and couldn't shake the strange sensation that I wasn't entirely present, that only Nathan and Stephen fully occupied the room.

Although I had no idea what I wanted to do, I told them that I intended to drive into town later. "No beach for me today."

"We can go with you," Stephen offered.

"Yeah, Mom."

"No, that's okay. You two have fun. I'll pick up something for dinner."

—

After they left in Stephen's car, I wondered afresh what had miraculously flipped Nathan's animosity to affability. I cleaned the breakfast dishes, closed the open windows, switched on the air conditioning, and returned to the bedroom, vaguely uneasy, though I didn't know why except to acknowledge an ominous presentiment coloring my mood. To distract myself, I checked my cell phone. To my surprise, Melissa had called. This was somewhat unusual even while she was living with Nathan; now, my curiosity was piqued, especially after I heard the message: "Bess, I'd like to speak with you about Nathan."

Melissa was an attractive, dark-haired, petite Asian-American with alert brown eyes; smart, well educated, kind, and capable, with a responsible management position at a large bank. Hugh and I had become very attached to her and had been optimistic that she would become our daughter-in-law. Although I had enjoyed speaking with Melissa in the past, at present, I was worried that she might launch into a litany of my son's faults, even if this wasn't her style. Yet I also believed it was only right to give her a chance to explain, to listen to her perspective. And, if she provided an explanation as to why their relationship had failed, those insights might prove useful.

She picked up on the fourth ring and sounded friendly, as she always had. After inquiring about my health, to which I gave a perfunctory reply, Melissa began prefacing her remarks with statements to the effect that she was reluctant to talk about Nathan, to go behind his back in order to communicate with me.

"Nathan told me your relationship ended. I'm sure you're very disappointed. I am too."

"Did he say why?" she asked.

"I'd like to hear your side, if you're willing to share it."

"I'll tell you one of the reasons I broke up with him. Not the second. Is that all right?"

I took note of this remark but respected her conditions. "Yes. Whatever you're comfortable doing."

"Okay. Well, a few weeks ago, we were discussing marriage. Or, rather, I was. I'm thirty-four and really want to have a child. I asked Nathan about taking these next steps, but he put me off. A night later, however, he declared that he was against getting married and didn't want to be a father. As you can imagine, I was stunned. When I pressed him, Nathan grew defensive, then angry and stormed out of the apartment. He sometimes gets annoyed or goes quiet, but he doesn't lose his temper to this degree, so I decided he was struggling with a serious issue."

Considering Nathan's behavior here, Melissa's report of her experience was pertinent. "I would come to the same conclusion."

"I thought about his reaction for a while and planned a special dinner for that weekend. To see if I could get Nathan to confide why he'd been so adamant." Melissa hesitated, which I noticed with mounting trepidation. "Anyway, we drank some wine—in fact, he had quite a lot of wine—until he admitted what was bothering him." She paused, leaving me in nervous suspense."

"What was it?"

"Nathan doesn't want to pass on the BRCA2 gene."

"But he's never been tested."

"That's what I thought," Melissa replied. "Not true. He went to New York without telling me—"

I inhaled sharply, knowing what Melissa would say next. "Nor me."

"Nathan does have the gene mutation. That's why he doesn't

want to risk having a child who might inherit it." Melissa waited for me to take this in. "And he's terrified about the increased likelihood of getting cancer himself."

My heart slammed to a stop. I dropped my head into my hand and felt sick. Oh, how I'd hoped that Nathan would be lucky, would beat the fifty-fifty odds! It was excruciating to imagine him anxiously waiting for the first tumors to appear, fretting over every doctor's appointment and every lump, pain, or bout of indigestion. What torture it would be to live with this fear! And I would be gone by then, when the cancer began its insidious attack. Unable to support my son when he needed me the most. Even Melissa wouldn't be there.

"Are you all right, Bess?" Melissa asked.

"I don't know." I couldn't disguise my shock and fell silent again, struggling to comprehend the enormity of Nathan's potential death sentence. Although my mind insisted I was being irrational, I couldn't help feeling guilty for passing this horrible affliction to my son. My father had most likely died due to BRCA2, though the genetic mutation hadn't been discovered until recently, and I would die from it too. Now Nathan might follow us, his life shortened like ours.

"I'm sorry, Melissa," I said at last. "I wasn't expecting this. Nathan just told me he wasn't sure about taking the test. Of course, I asked him to do so. Several times. I wanted him to be alert…for his doctors to know…" I sounded like I wasn't making any sense.

"Bess, maybe it wasn't right to break Nathan's confidence, but I thought you should be aware of the results so you're prepared when he tells you. And I'm sure he will when he's ready. There's no one else he loves and trusts as much as you. No one. And, considering our separation, he isn't going to turn to me again."

"I understand. Thank you, Melissa."

"And, if at all possible—and this might be asking a lot—I'd prefer that you don't mention this conversation to Nathan. It might jeopardize whatever friendship we still have."

"No, I won't. Not unless it's…well, I'll try not to." My voice was flat, lifeless. After clearing my throat, I said, "I'm sorry things didn't work out between the two of you. I had great hopes. You'll find someone as special as you are, Melissa. I'm sure of that."

We ended the call a few minutes later. In a daze, I lay down on the bed, wishing to hide under the covers and never emerge. Although my own imminent death was frightening, knowing Nathan might one day be in a similar state, possibly alone, was intolerable to bear. And because Melissa had requested for me to wait until he broached the subject, thus handing off her responsibility and exiting, this left me to absorb this onerous news without any way to relieve the burden. While her desire to do so was understandable, she had placed me in the familiar role as a depository of pain. More anguish for the cancer to feed upon.

Tears fell from my eyes and I began sobbing.

—

Some time later, my phone rang. I wiped my damp face and answered, though I really didn't want to talk with anyone. Especially not Hugh, but, alas, it was my husband.

"Bess, I was waiting. You promised you'd telephone."

"No, I didn't." I heard the thickness in my voice and knew Hugh would notice it. We'd been together too many years.

"What's wrong? Are you okay?"

I reached for a tissue and quickly blew my nose. "Yes. You just caught me at a bad moment." This lame excuse wouldn't deter him and it didn't.

"Bad because you don't feel well or because you're unhappy?"

I felt a strong urge to share Nathan's BRCA2 gene test with Hugh. Under normal circumstances, he would have been the first person I would have told. Although he deserved to know, I'd heard the results from Melissa, who had requested my discretion. If Hugh became upset and contacted Nathan directly, Nathan would be furious with Melissa and probably with me.

"A little of both, I suppose. Constipation, as usual." I avoided the emotional part of what was wrong. Hugh was usually satisfied with a discussion of physical issues and less comfortable with talking about how I was feeling.

"I'm sorry to hear that, dear," he replied. "Bess, you know I worry about you. I really do." This sounded genuine, reminding me of why I still cared about Hugh.

"I'll be fine."

He asked when I was coming home, which I didn't answer. He would learn soon enough that his world was about to collapse.

"Please, Bess, I miss you. If you're angry with me or concerned about something I did, can't we talk about it? I'll drive to wherever you are. We'll have a glass of wine and a nice dinner and—"

"No, not now, Hugh. I think we both need some time apart. We'll talk soon." I said goodbye and ended the connection before he could press for details or complain about household matters such as the laundry.

The call hadn't improved my mood, nor was I feeling well. In the bathroom, I finally found a little relief from the pile-up in my intestines. The effort left me shaky and overheated, but I scrubbed my face, applied some makeup, slipped on shorts and a blouse, and forced myself to leave the house, with the intention of driving to town after a detour to check the beach where I'd met Stephen, in case Nathan and Stephen were there. In my weakened state, I didn't relish tackling the dunes, but my compulsion to see my son—even from afar—was overwhelming.

—

The temperature was rising to ninety-one degrees, according to the radio forecast. Too warm for me to be on the beach in my present condition, but when I came across Stephen's white sedan, my irrational anxiety to check that my son was all right overcame common sense. I started trudging up the high dune, feeling perspiration break out on my forehead, and the hot sun scorch my skin. At the crest, my eyes blurred and the heat transformed the scene into an unnatural infrared image, as if everything was electrified and pulsing with light. I lowered my sunglasses and blinked several times to normalize my vision before scanning the broad beach, which was speckled with people sun-tanning on blankets. On the first pass, I missed Nathan and Stephen until Stephen rose to his elbow, leaned on his towel, and the sun illuminated his white hair. He twisted to his left and hovered over Nathan, who was lying on a towel beside him. My first reaction was relief, seeing that the two were getting along, but as I continued to watch, Nathan reached up and pulled Stephen's head down to his. They exchanged a long kiss and fell into each other's arms.

My jaw dropped and I stood there, shocked. "Oh, my god," I whispered, staring at the two men twisting together. Was that really Stephen? But no one else had white hair and his magnificent physique. And, like any mother, I could recognize my son easily, despite the distance.

My feet felt rooted to the spot, but then I panicked, afraid that Stephen or Nathan would see me. I spun around, desperate to escape so I could absorb this stunning news in the privacy of my car. Half running down the dune, I suddenly felt faint. Before I could catch my balance, my knees buckled and I tumbled sideways in the sand.

14

I must have been unconscious for a few seconds. When I opened my eyes, I was disoriented and couldn't recall falling, yet I was lying face down on the sand. My cheek stung and felt scuffed as did my bare knee. I raised myself to a sitting position, and slowly my memory fell into place, scene by scene: the beach, Stephen, Nathan, and the kiss. Still dizzy, I brushed sand from my face, arms, and legs; reached for my sunglasses that were hooked on a goldenrod plant and put them on, grateful to have the harsh sun partially blocked by the dark green lenses. I came to my feet, remained stationary for a few seconds until my balance stabilized, and then gingerly descended the hill and walked to my car. When I squeezed the door-opener button, my hand was trembling.

Inside, I sprawled against the seat, shaken from the fall and by what I'd witnessed. Was this Nathan's first time with a gay guy? I knew how irresistible Stephen was and could certainly empathize with anyone—male or female—who would be attracted to him. Or was this affair with Stephen one of many? Had Nathan lied about being heterosexual to disguise his orientation? I found that hard to believe, yet Melissa had mentioned a second reason she and Nathan were ending their relationship. Perhaps she had discovered his interest in men, which would have been a blow on several levels: unfaithfulness primarily, but also a fear of sexually transmitted diseases if Nathan had been with multiple partners.

I switched on the ignition, set the air-conditioner on high, and considered Nathan's boyhood: all the times Hugh had derided Nathan for being soft, for refusing to play contact sports, for demonstrating insufficient enthusiasm about dating. Not that Hugh was a macho jock by any means, but he was determined to raise his son to be successful with the opposite sex. Observing Nathan's discomfort with all this pressure and the resentment that was growing between father and son, I had encouraged Nathan to pursue interests he preferred: drawing classes, theater, band, school track meets, and local marathon races. Although it had never occurred to me that Nathan might be gay, there were signals I might have missed, signals that Hugh may have perceived consciously or unconsciously, causing him to try steering Nathan away from his true nature. On the night when Hugh spoke to him about his offensive behavior with David and Paul, perhaps Hugh had chided Nathan for rudeness but sympathized with his discomfort in order to put Nathan at ease. However, if Nathan had been acting out only because of his own sexual confusion, hearing anti-gay comments might have driven Nathan to conceal his homosexuality even more carefully. And if Nathan thought Hugh was biased, it would add to his animosity toward his father. One thing I was sure about: unless he was really distressed on the evening when David and Paul visited, Nathan wouldn't have confessed to being gay during the conversation with his father. I was also positive he would never talk to Hugh before confiding in me. And if he had, Hugh would have told me immediately.

I thought of the misery Nathan had possibly endured all these years, misery I might have relieved, and felt heartbroken. Unless the relationship with Stephen was a first-time homosexual encounter, I had been woefully unaware of my son's secret and had failed to help Nathan find confidence within himself. And Hugh, if calmly approached about his son's orientation, would also have rallied to support him.

I wanted to call my husband to confide what I had learned, but I didn't. Nathan was responsible for telling both of us in his own time, in his own way, although it would be difficult to hide his relationship with Stephen from me, considering the confines of the small cottage. His truth would probably be revealed very soon, either by accident or by deliberate disclosure. Although the two men had obviously been intimate with each other last night, until they were ready to be open, I wouldn't confront them.

And then there was my own dilemma with Stephen. As much as I wanted Nathan to be with someone, my relationship with Stephen seemed like a life preserver that had been tossed my way, a bright miracle in a dark time. Even if I had ended the sexual part, I hadn't intended to conclude the intimacy, though my restrictions were selfish and hadn't taken into account what Stephen wanted. Now the quandary had grown complex: how to reconcile my needs with my son's and Stephen's. I had to admit losing the closeness with Stephen pained me deeply, yet the speed with which Stephen had moved on to Nathan, as if I had only been a meaningless fling, really stung. But Nathan came first, always had, and always would.

Replaying the scene on the beach, I drove into Provincetown, wrestling with confusion as well as questioning my idea of buying special gifts for both men, which I'd planned as an acknowledgment of their kindness.

With good luck, I located a parking space on Commercial Street but remained in the car. Should I return to the house because my back ached or stay in town and follow through on my intention? Finally, I dabbed some makeup on my face, locked the car, and began wandering around the galleries, jewelry stores, and shops. The sparkling lights on the glass counters and the intense colors on the displayed items dazzled my eyes, blending everything into a kaleidoscope of reflections and hues. After twenty minutes, I was forced to rest on a bench. As if in slow motion, men and women strolled past, most of them gay, many in couples. How happy they looked, no doubt relieved to be in a place where they were free to celebrate their love. I smiled to see this and hoped my son, if like them, was as delighted with Stephen.

Once I recovered, I entered a jewelry shop and perused the watches, rings, and necklaces. A handsome gold and copper cuff bracelet caught my attention; its gleaming copper resembled the color of Nathan's hair. It was expensive, but I decided to buy it. The salesmen wrapped the bracelet with silver paper and purple ribbon.

Having purchased a present for Nathan, I needed to do the same for Stephen. Something other than jewelry because jewelry wasn't appropriate for our relationship, whatever it was. In a men's shop, I found a white crewneck cotton sweater with raglan sleeves that seemed like something Stephen would wear. The man behind the counter explained that it was cut long, which would suit anyone Stephen's height. This, too, was wrapped.

Exhausted as I was after my outing, I was pleased with the gifts. I drove to Truro and bought three cooked lobsters and New England clam chowder. Although the yellow corn looked appealing, I decided my intestines didn't need additional punishment, so I opted for potato salad and ripe tomatoes. For tomorrow's lunch, I purchased three Kaiser rolls, a wedge of Brie, a can of cranberry sauce, and a pound of sliced turkey.

—

After storing the groceries, I walked into the bathroom and rigorously scoured my hands with soap and hot water. I always did this after touching surfaces that might contain germs, such as coins and bills, which were heavily contaminated. Dr. Melbourne had warned me about becoming sick, though a warning wasn't necessary—I was already phobic, carrying a small bottle of hand sanitizer everywhere.

I dried my fingers and studied the abrasions on my cheek and leg. I could hide one with trousers, but even covered with liquid makeup, the redness remained visible on the side of my face. I didn't want to admit I'd been to the beach, though I hadn't been spying, just anxious, nor was I comfortable saying I'd fallen because that would worry Nathan and Stephen. What other explanation could I offer? I decided to let the situation dictate my response.

I ate at one o'clock. A half of a sandwich, which was half of a sandwich too much. My stomach roiling, I sat in the kitchen, sank my head in my hands. How would I handle the return to Stamford? Could I drive home if Nathan broke his promise and went with Stephen to Boston? I was suddenly less confident about making the trip alone because of the increased pain, the extra fentanyl dose, and the few bouts of dizziness I'd experienced. Although I'd been more or less okay driving to and from town, my reactions hadn't been tested at highway speeds or at a distance of two-hundred-and-fifty miles.

I raised my eyes to the window and fought back tears.

—

When Stephen and Nathan entered the house several hours later, the sexual vibration between them crackled through the air. They stood nearer to each other than two men commonly did, a closing of the physical space that confirmed their union. I also noticed that their shirts were disheveled, which wasn't typical of either of them, and their clothes appeared dry. Had they removed their bathing trunks in the car? And what else had happened when they did? I quickly erased this unwanted image from my mind.

They both gave me large smiles, Nathan's more of a wide grin.

"So, did you have fun at the beach?" I asked.

"We did!" Nathan said with atypical enthusiasm.

As Stephen approached, I experienced a strange surge of desire, as if the magnetism between them was contagious. Even in the dusky room, Stephen glowed, invigorated from the sun and sea and perhaps Nathan's adoration. I reminded myself that I had already drawn a line with him, and the fact of his new relationship with my son drew a double underscore. Stephen was no longer my lover—my decision—and coveting him seemed suspiciously tinged with envy. Now that I couldn't have Stephen, did I want him? Or was I upset that Nathan's attentions had shifted to Stephen, when Nathan was visiting to be with me? My reaction, whatever the cause, felt vaguely sickening, perhaps even remotely incestuous, as

I considered that I had shared the same lover with my son within twenty-four hours. Even if I hadn't created this triangle, Nathan had known what had happened with Stephen, and Stephen—the man in the middle—had either acceded to Nathan's advances or seduced him.

Nathan kissed me with the same lips he'd likely kissed Stephen in the car a few minutes before. And he didn't notice the scuff marks on my face, which Stephen did as he neared.

He touched the red area gently. "What's this?"

"Nothing. I tripped and fell. I'm fine."

Stephen raised his eyebrow. "Have you been losing your balance often?"

"No, not really."

"Hmm, well, we'll have to keep watch on you." He gave me a mock-stern look, smiled, and joined Nathan in the kitchen.

Despite all the mental turmoil, I couldn't stop my response to Stephen. It was impossible not to be attracted to him. Was he aware of his irresistible effect? Or was he using his charisma to lure people and for what purpose? Did he feed off his conquests in an attempt to fill a hole left by being an unwanted child who had been abandoned in an orphanage?

I sat in the armchair by the sofa and reflected on Stephen's comment that his friends thought he could find a replacement for Terry without any effort and how misunderstood that made him feel. If true, how could Stephen enter into another relationship so soon—first with me and then with Nathan? He had portrayed himself as still in mourning and cried over Terry's loss, yet he had become involved with us, allowing only hours between Nathan and myself. How many other affairs had come before? Was Stephen a superficial, gorgeous stud with no feelings, a high-functioning sociopath, or was he in need of emotional support, attempting to find connection through physical liaisons, through the very activities his friends had suggested?

I sighed. Stephen was not a heartless sociopath. He exhibited real empathy and caring. I needed to stanch my attraction to him and let the two men decide what should happen when the lights were turned off tonight.

Nathan and Stephen were murmuring in the kitchen, probably so I couldn't hear what they were saying. My son came into the living room first.

"Bought some more white wine, Mom. I know you're not drinking much these days, but at least you'll have a selection."

"Thank you, dear. And, as you may have noticed, lobsters are for dinner."

"Excellent! I love lobster!" Stephen exclaimed, walking toward the other armchair and lowering himself into it. "Also saw some chowder. Quite a feast, Bess." His mouth formed into a lopsided, boyish grin that was eerily reminiscent of Nathan's smile.

My son sprawled on the sofa and crossed his legs toward Stephen. I couldn't remember when Nathan had looked so joyful. It was as if he had absorbed Stephen's sunniness, humor, and optimism, qualities I didn't equate with Nathan, who tended to be somber, dry-witted, and ironic. While I was delighted to see my son in such a great mood, I worried that Stephen wasn't committed to their relationship, that he might consider it a dalliance that had arisen suddenly and would disappear just as suddenly, as Stephen himself might. Nathan, on the other hand, appeared to be hypnotized, barely containing his delight. In most cases, I would celebrate his pleasure, but I'd just been in bed with the man and was still a little infatuated, if a mature woman could claim that.

"How was the water?" I asked.

"Chilly," said Nathan.

"Perfect," said Stephen.

They laughed and recounted details of their day. Their tandem descriptions reminded me of the amazing conversational smoothness I'd experienced with Stephen. Watching Nathan, I also noticed how he tried to disguise his fascination with Stephen by turning away, yet each time the pull was too great, and he faced him again.

After a few minutes of this dialogue, my son asked me if I wanted a glass of wine.

"Okay," I agreed, though I was still unsettled from the intestinal battles earlier, nor had the pain lessened.

Nathan rose, slipped between the coffee table and Stephen's legs, dropping his palm on Stephen's bare knee as if for balance, and then strode into the kitchen. I stared at Stephen, waiting for an explanation.

He returned my gaze, his eyes crinkling with quiet amusement. "So, Bess, did you fall on the sand dune?"

"What?"

He smiled. "The dune. You know where and when."

My mouth fell open. I closed it, but it was too late to hide my surprise. "You saw me?"

"There? Yes."

I couldn't imagine how he had since he was otherwise engaged with Nathan, and I had descended the hill seconds after the kiss. Nor had he been looking in my direction before the two had come together, or at least I didn't think so.

"I lost my balance as I was returning to the car."

"Because of what you observed?"

Stephen was being coy. "No. I get lightheaded sometimes." After saying this, I remembered that I had just denied having issues with my balance.

"And this was one of those times?"

"It was." I felt like crossing my arms, but I was determined to appear unflustered. "I'll leave it to you and Nathan…to tell me what's going on."

"Okay. Or rather Nathan should."

I nodded and felt distinctly uncomfortable with Stephen's indifferent attitude about his sexual liaison with my son. A wave of maternal protectiveness swept over me.

"Why did you do it?" I asked, unable to stop myself.

"I have my reasons." Stephen gave me a patient look. "Are you upset?"

Before I could reply or ask for a clearer explanation, Nathan came in with three glasses and a bottle tucked under his arm.

"Let's sit outside," he said. "It's a beautiful evening."

Stephen stood. I did the same and followed the two men through the screen door to the patio. Nathan poured the wine, and we took chairs at the table—Nathan across from me and Stephen on my right. As the late afternoon sun shone on him, Stephen's beauty was on full display. He leaned back, folded one long, muscled leg over the other, and gave every appearance of being relaxed and content. Yet something about his casual expression was contrived, almost artificial. Surely he must be worried about what would occur later, when the music stopped, and the three of us had to choose a bed for the night? And what about Nathan? He was smiling constantly, his eyes were too bright, and he kept sending warm glances at Stephen. Had the two made a pact between them as to where Stephen would sleep?

I resolved to remain calm, but I sensed the tension between the three of us, the hemmed-in compression that even sitting out of doors, under the open sky, couldn't diminish. I sipped my wine and waited, trying to absorb the stillness that had arrived with the advent of evening, and failed.

—

After the chowder, I ate my one-pound lobster and immediately wished I hadn't. The food landed heavily, more like liquid cement than shellfish. Stephen and Nathan polished off their two-pounders as well as everything else on their plates. After we cleaned the dishes and returned outside, Stephen lit some citronella candles to discourage mosquitoes, topped off his glass and Nathan's, and then gave me a big smile.

"Bess, dinner was a very special treat. Thank you."

Nathan, not to be outdone on politeness, chimed in with similar comments. I noted how my son sought to imitate Stephen's manners, which were impeccable, but that he was slow to initiate gracious compliments and sometimes exhibited insensitivity to-ward others. Watching his interactions, I was also struck by how self-conscious Nathan was, how he had developed a defensive posture, unlike Stephen, who radiated approachability, friendliness, and confidence through firm eye contact and physical openness—shoulders back and head held high. Stephen had mastered the art of filling his own personal space without encroaching on anyone's boundaries. Nathan didn't do either well. This observation made me wonder if my son's distrustfulness was a reaction to years of Hugh's criticism, which I might have more forcefully prevented.

"I have something for both of you," I said, rising to my feet.

"Presents?" Stephen asked, smiling.

"Yes. Just a minute."

I walked into the kitchen and glanced at the two men through the window. They were leaning in toward each other, whispering. I felt excluded, as if they were eager for me to leave their company so they could be alone. Perhaps this was an unreasonable impression, but our complicated triangular situation required untangling—and soon.

In the studio, I removed the two packages from a metal cabinet where I'd hidden them. When I turned, I noticed that the blue artist's smock that had been draped over the back of the sofa was now folded on the metal stool. Had Stephen and Nathan used the couch last night? I could think of no other explanation. And, afterward, did Stephen return to my bed, acting as if nothing had occurred with my son? If so, was this done out of concern for my feelings or to hide their sexual encounter? In either case, I felt deceived.

I took a deep breath, rolled my shoulders to relax the accumulated tension, and carried the presents outside, handing the smaller box to Nathan and the larger one to Stephen. Then I sat down and watched Nathan unwrap his first, ripping the paper in a hurry, as he always did. The bracelet fit his wrist perfectly.

He bent toward me and kissed my forehead. "I love it, Mom!"

Stephen opened his gift next and pulled the sweater over his sports shirt. "This is perfect, Bess! It's beautifully made and just the right size. Thank you."

I was relieved that both presents had been well chosen, yet I couldn't shake my distress. The gift-giving now felt forced, as if I had been trying too hard to please both men or else that I wanted something in exchange. Marcel Mauss, in a seminal 1924 work, had written that the offering of gifts imposed an implied debt of reciprocity. I had intended them to be a thank-you for their support, without any presumption that further obligations were expected. However, the giving might stem from a subconscious wish to make the two feel guilty: being generous to them in contrast to their rejection of me. I hoped not.

Between being ill from dinner and being disappointed in Nathan's lack of candor regarding Stephen, I wished to retreat into the bedroom and close the door. But as I was about to stand, Nathan peeked at Stephen, who nodded, as if in encouragement.

Addressing me, Nathan said, "Mom, there's something I need to tell you."

Even though I didn't want it, I drank some wine. "Yes, Nathan?"

15

"I should have been honest with you years ago," Nathan began, "but I figured if I told you, you would tell Dad. And then he'd get on me about what a disappointment I was. Anyway, now that you're divorcing him, maybe it'll be easier for you to keep my confidence."

I watched how nervous my son had become and felt troubled that he hadn't trusted me enough to discuss his homosexuality before, if that was the issue on his mind. "Nathan, if you'd asked, I wouldn't have relayed our conversation to Hugh. You know that."

He hung his head. "I'm sorry, Mom. You've always been fair with me. I guess I was too afraid of Dad…how he might react."

"You and I could sit down with Hugh and talk," I said, frustrated by his evasiveness.

"No, I'm not ready for that." His face tensed and he shifted in his chair. After a deep breath, he said, "I'm gay."

"Gay?" I was taken aback by the suddenness of his announcement after the circuitous preamble. "How long have you known?"

"Since I was twelve."

The fact that Nathan had been grappling with his sexuality for all these years was a surprise. All I could manage was to repeat what he said. "Since twelve?"

Nathan nodded. "Did you know? I mean, when I was growing up?"

"No, I didn't."

He gave me a small smile, as if relieved that the deception had been successful. "And Dad?"

"Not that he's ever said." While it was true that we hadn't spoken about this possibility, I wondered for a second time if Hugh had been more perceptive about Nathan than I had.

Nathan glanced at Stephen before resuming his story. "I didn't have any experiences until my sophomore year in college, though I wanted to."

"I thought you had some steady girlfriends then."

"Yeah, well, I did date a little, but mostly I made up women to keep Dad from bugging me," Nathan said. "My first real gay relationship was after I moved to SoHo. Erich was a journalist, a really great guy. I thought I'd finally found the right man. Someone I could bring home."

"What happened?" I asked.

"He was assigned to Berlin and fell in love."

"I'm so sorry, Nathan."

"Well, yeah, it was awful. I was really depressed and had no one to talk to about it."

He could have spoken with me. Why hadn't he? "Did you ever see him again?"

"Once. Years later when he came to the city on business. But it was over…the relationship." He stared at the sky, as if to compose himself before continuing. "After Erich, I decided to try dating women again. I went out with a couple of girls—a lot, actually. But I kept going to gay bars in between. And then I met Melissa. I was sure we could make it. The sex was okay—good enough—and I liked everything about her."

"I did too," I agreed.

"Even though I cared for Melissa, after a few months, I couldn't stop myself from hooking up with guys again. Telling Melissa I was working late or having dinner with clients. Mom, I hated myself. I felt just like Dad, with all of his slimy lies. How I could do this to her? After I'd watched how Dad hurt you…oh, god! And how was I going to tell you that I was gay when you liked Melissa so much?" Nathan rubbed his thigh. "I know you and Dad expected us to marry. But when I started deceiving her, there was no way to reveal my sexual orientation without admitting what I'd been doing. And marriage? I couldn't vow to be faithful." Nathan thrust his head on his hand, his face wreathed in misery.

I asked if Melissa had known about the men in Nathan's life.

My son looked at Stephen, as if to gauge his reaction. Stephen swallowed some wine and made no comment.

"Not until the end," Nathan replied. "When I refused to marry her."

Ever since seeing the two on the beach, I'd had time to adjust to the revelation that he was gay, but as the hours passed, I'd become more disturbed by my lack of perception, my blindness to the chasm that existed between us. In my practice, I had often noted that people were essentially unknowable; I had never expected this to be true of my own child. And now, learning that Nathan had behaved like Hugh—cheating and lying—was another weighty matter. Perhaps, due to vanity, I had believed my son's personality was like mine, yet his dishonesty with Melissa was right out of Hugh's playbook, and concocting heterosexual relationships that didn't exist would even trouble Hugh. If Hugh and I had espoused prejudice, I might sympathize with Nathan's reluctance to be truthful, but we were liberal parents, and while I was certain my husband would react positively as soon as he digested the news, he would feel dismayed about Nathan's attempts to hide his sexuality. Using our potential disapproval as an excuse for the deception would also strike Hugh as unfair, as it did me.

—

"Nathan, I don't care if you're gay. That would never, never have been a problem. You know that I've had gay clients and colleagues. If you had brought your partner home, we would have welcomed him."

"Even Dad?" Nathan narrowed his eyes.

"If you had asked me to speak with Hugh on your behalf, I would've done so. However, that wouldn't have been necessary nor is it necessary now. He might be a little upset at first—surprised might be more accurate—but he's open-minded and would have accepted you. Your father loves you and cares that you're happy."

"He has a weird way of showing it."

"That doesn't mean what I said is untrue. I think you're allowing your bitterness toward him to discredit his good attributes. Conferring bias where there isn't any. Nathan, talk with your father—not when we arrive because he's going to be in a state about the divorce, but shortly after."

Nathan played with his wine glass, moving it in small, agitated circles. "Okay, I will. I don't have anything to lose, but he does."

I was saddened by this poorly veiled threat to sever ties with his father if Hugh didn't behave exactly as Nathan wished. Hugh would need his son during the coming months and as he grew older, and Nathan would need Hugh to support him after I was gone. Unfortunately, I couldn't help the two of them work through their differences. I could only hope they would retreat from their separate corners and reconnect.

When Nathan looked away from me and focused on Stephen again, I assumed he was wondering if the relationship with Stephen was solid, if Stephen was the man he could introduce to Hugh. Stephen, my one-night, one-morning lover.

Stephen took another sip of wine, dried his lips with a napkin, and smiled at Nathan. "Glad you told Bess."

"Yes, I am too," I replied, trying to ignore my disillusionment. "Nathan, I understand how upset you are about Melissa and that you feel like your actions were similar to your father's. While I agree with you in principle, your reasons were different." I paused, searching for a diplomatic way to communicate my opinion, one that wouldn't antagonize my son. "What concerns me is that you were trying to lie to yourself. To pretend you were heterosexual because of the pressure you felt about conforming to social expectations—"

"And Dad's," Nathan inserted.

"Your father will be fine." I extended my hand across the table and took his. "But it hurts to know that you suffered through so many conflicts and struggled for such a long time by yourself. It must have been very painful. More recently, did you have some friends to talk to?"

"A few."

"I'm glad of that," I replied, squeezing his fingers. "And as for Melissa, I'm sure admitting everything to her was hard. I know how much you care about her."

"I do. We've had several conversations since she found out, and I've apologized. My hope is that we can remain friends, but that's her decision."

"Good that you've talked with each other. I hope you stay connected. She's a lovely person."

Suddenly, I felt exhausted. And discouraged. Regardless of all my efforts to be a loving parent, I had failed to earn Nathan's trust, as, in a way, he had also failed me. I didn't know if I had the strength to bridge the gulf between us, one I'd never dreamed existed before, but I needed to try.

Nathan withdrew his hand from mine and refilled his glass. After drinking some wine, he began recounting details about his teenage doubts and anxieties, his first attractions to men, none of which I'd noticed, much to my consternation. While my son had covered his feelings well, I accused myself of heterosexual chauvinism, of tacitly assuming Nathan was straight. Even so, as I listened to his accounts of subterfuges and pretenses, I wished that I'd cultivated more integrity in him.

Once he had laid out his history, Nathan paused and directed his attention to Stephen. "Okay if I tell her?"

Stephen shrugged. "Think she already knows, Nathan."

My son looked at me, astonished. "Do you?"

"About you and Stephen?" I nodded. "Yes."

"So you let me go on and on about being gay and didn't say anything?" he demanded.

"It was your place to tell me, not my place to ask."

Nathan's posture stiffened. From our many talks over the years, he knew this was how I conducted myself, yet he was annoyed. "I don't care, Mom. You could have made it a hell of a lot easier! About telling you."

"I've always tried to respect your privacy."

Suddenly, his face darkened. "Respect *my* privacy?" He drew his hand into a fist and banged it against the table. "What a stupid platitude! It's *your* privacy you're worried about, not mine. It's you who needed to wall yourself off. Like you did with Dad—so you didn't have to confront him about his affairs and could keep pretending everything was okay. If you had any self-respect, you would have left him years ago." He said this angrily, but then his tone changed. More plaintively, he asked, "And why didn't you stand up for me against Dad?"

"I did."

Nathan shook his head. "Not very often! How many times did you walk away when Dad and I were fighting? Or when I came to you for help, and you told me to work things out with my father, that we needed to resolve our own problems. You just said that again a minute ago!"

"What's wrong with that? I stepped in when I thought I should. I was respecting—"

"You weren't respecting me, you were protecting yourself. So you could keep your distance. Stay calm and collected. Well, I'm tired of that and your therapist's speeches! Lose your cool and be a human!" He took a gulp of wine and stared at me, his eyes smoldering.

"Is there more?" My voice was on the edge of cracking.

Nathan snorted. "See what I mean? For god's sake, get mad! You told me you were going to be open about how you're feeling… not pretend everything is always okay and under control. So, when is that new program going into effect, Mom? Huh? You know, the one where we're friends and not mother and son? Or was that all a load of crap?"

"I think Bess did the right thing," Stephen cut in. "Waiting for you to tell your story."

Nathan shot a look at Stephen. "Yeah, technically that might be true. She's always technically perfect."

I was astounded by the depth of my son's hostility. "Was this why you didn't tell me you were gay? Because you didn't feel close?"

His mouth tightened. "Yes."

I exhaled a long breath, and as the air left my lungs, the pain radiated across my back, overpowering my ability to think clearly. Lowering my head, I tried to concentrate, to banish the physical distractions and to talk myself into a civil response and couldn't. I was too wounded by his harsh words.

"You're right, Nathan. I promised to be open with you. About how I feel." I lifted my eyes to his, saw his anger, which ignited my own. "Well, if you really want to know, I feel absolutely rotten. I'm sorry if I distanced myself from you—that was the last thing on earth I intended. Our relationship means everything to me, and I'll do whatever it takes to repair it." I struggled to maintain my usual restraint and lost the fight. "But what about you? Didn't you come to Provincetown to help me? Didn't you say my life was more important than yours right now? And didn't I tell you how much Stephen's kindness and caring meant? You forgot all that, didn't you? You insisted that I shouldn't sleep with him because you couldn't tolerate us in the same bed together, yet when you told me this, you were hoping to seduce Stephen yourself. How is that putting me first? That is putting yourself first! What hypocrisy! What selfishness! Not only do you ignore your promise to me, you also take away someone I care about, someone who has made me happy." I thrust against my chair and grabbed my napkin to hide my shaking hands. "I am appalled by your behavior."

"I'm sorry about what happened, Bess," Stephen whispered.

I glanced at him. "Thank you." I focused on my son and waited.

Nathan's lips wrenched into various contortions as a series of feelings played across his face. After a quick peek at Stephen, he raised his glass. "Hear, hear." He drank some wine, rolled it around in his mouth, and swallowed. "Mom finally uncorks."

My cheeks warmed. "There is no need to be nasty."

Stephen spread his palms flat on the table, as if trying to physically tamp down the discord. "Relax, Nathan, and let this go."

Nathan raised his eyebrows, surprised that Stephen was intervening on my behalf. He was about to protest, but he gritted his teeth and sat there, fuming.

The air seemed to warp between the three of us as pulsing waves of red anger emanated from Nathan, silhouetting his body and charging outward, colliding with my own hot energy. I placed the napkin in my lap and tried to ease my ragged breathing and the fierce tightness in my back.

Nathan looked at us and appeared to be constructing another outburst. Perhaps sensing this, Stephen treated Nathan to a gentle, supportive smile. The soothing effect on my son was almost instantaneous.

I appreciated Stephen's diplomatic intervention and realized no one had addressed his feelings. "I'm sorry you're in the middle of this, Stephen," I said. "And that I haven't asked what you want."

The faint smile remained on his face. "From Nathan or from you?"

"Both."

He looked away, his eyes surveying the flowers in the garden and the dark sky until they eventually settled on me again. "I want everyone to get along. To love and care for each other."

This unexpectedly mild response took me aback. It neither affirmed our connection or his with Nathan. Tucked inside the words might be a subtle admonishment, but I couldn't tell which of us he was chastising or if he was merely being tactful.

"I want that too," I replied.

Nathan rolled his new bracelet around his wrist. As if this movement reset his mood, Nathan managed a crooked smile. In a low voice, he said, "Yeah. I agree. Mom, I meant what I said about helping you."

"I know you did, Nathan. And I do need your help."

My son acknowledged this with a nod. And then—perhaps as a peace offering—he refilled my glass halfway. We sat in silence, the night falling around us, the candle's flame swaying in the breeze. I tried to think of a safe topic, but nothing seemed safe anymore. After several minutes, Nathan looked at Stephen.

"So, when did you know you were gay? How old were you?"

Stephen blinked, as if he had woken from a trance, and thrust a forefinger against his chest. "Me? Hey, what's the old line? I'm not gay, I'm happy?" He laughed lightly, but seeing Nathan's displeasure, he stopped. "Well, that's sort of true in my case, though I lean gay. Remember? I don't like labels."

I noted Nathan's reaction. Clearly, he wasn't amused with Stephen's ambiguous answer.

"Huh? What are you saying?" he asked Stephen.

"Nothing, really. I just see sexuality as fluid and dependent on circumstances. The people involved. That doesn't mean I can't be loyal in a relationship. I married Terry, after all."

Nathan retreated into his chair as if Stephen had pushed him backward. Because I didn't know what had transpired between them, I wasn't sure if Nathan had leaped ahead, making assumptions about Stephen's interest that weren't accurate or were premature, that he was more invested in Stephen than Stephen was in him.

"And Stephen is also still grieving for Terry." Immediately after I uttered this reminder, I regretted it, knowing my comment had been prompted by Stephen's remark about being loyal and my disappointment over the fast switch he'd made from me to my son.

Nathan tossed a sour look in my direction and didn't respond.

Stephen didn't, either. Instead, he placed his hand on Nathan's arm, giving it a playful shake. "Hey, come on! Everything's all right."

For a second, I thought Nathan was going to cling to his irritation, but then his shoulders lowered and the tightness in his mouth relaxed. "Are you sure?"

"Of course!" Stephen laced his fingers through Nathan's. "Are we okay?"

Nathan cracked a weak smile. "Yeah, I guess."

Seeing the two men entwine their hands was unsettling. Not because of the gay issue, but because I still possessed feelings for Stephen and hadn't adjusted to the swift change in my relationship with him. In addition to this dilemma, I realized our dialogue hadn't clarified the bedroom arrangements. I hesitated to broach the subject, but I was growing weary and needed to retire soon.

As I was about to raise the matter, Nathan leaned over and kissed Stephen. The two hugged and then, recovered from his doubts, my son rose to his feet. "Hey, we need some chocolate!"

Stephen and I stared at each other as Nathan left to retrieve the box. For a second, I wished we could return to our first night together and obliterate everything else that had happened. But that was impossible, and I reproached myself for the tiny, treacherous impulse.

"So, are you sleeping in the guest room with Nathan?"

"I was wondering when you'd ask." He gave me an inscrutable smile. "I know what Nathan expects. He's going to be really disappointed if I don't stay with him. And you'll be disappointed if I do."

When I started to deny this, Stephen raised his hands. "Bess, you know that's true."

He had me there. I nodded in reluctant agreement. "But Nathan's happiness is more important"

He laughed. "To you, perhaps."

"And not to you?" I couldn't hide my astonishment.

"I'm not willing to make that call. And if Nathan examines the situation—your situation—he should place your needs ahead of his own—if most of his needs are also met."

"And what about your needs? You really didn't say what they are."

"Yes, I did." He observed me with his usual serenity.

I shook my head, perplexed. "So what are you proposing?"

"I stay with you until you fall asleep. Once you do, I'll join Nathan."

Before I could answer, Nathan bounded out of the house with a new bottle of wine and the chocolates. I ate one candy, picked up my glass, and stood.

"I'm going for a short walk," I told them.

"Do you want company?" Stephen asked.

"No, thanks. I won't be long."

16

In the kitchen, I dumped my wine in the sink and washed the glass. I then moved the plates and silverware from the counter into the dishwasher, relieved that there was little to clean because the lobsters and chowder had been pre-cooked. When I finished, I observed the two men on the patio. They were standing close together by the table. Candlelight brightened their white shirts and faces and created a golden enclosure within the dark background behind them. Nathan's arm was draped around Stephen's shoulder, and, though they were nearly identical in height, Nathan looked smaller, like a younger, weaker brother, and his gesture appeared awkward, nor did Stephen's friendly smile match Nathan's more passionate expression. I considered Stephen's suggested sleeping plans and sensed they reflected an ambivalence that should worry my son. Did it really matter to Stephen where he slept or with whom? As nice as Stephen was, there was an air of ephemerality about him that left me in doubt whether he was aligned with Nathan or if he had ever been truly aligned with anyone. Even if he had professed a past pledge to Terry, their relationship may not have been as committed as described.

Another significant issue was Stephen's handsomeness. Would he have too many opportunities to stray and would he behave like Hugh? All of his life, Nathan had dealt with the effects of unfaithfulness on me and secondarily on himself. Considering the Imago model, did Nathan's attraction to Stephen harken back to his father? Was my son unconsciously seeking men who were potentially adulterous, who would leave him in a role similar to my own?

I turned away from the window, saddened by all of these possibilities, though not about the news of Nathan's sexuality, yet the lack of character he had demonstrated by betraying Melissa was troubling. I loved my son, but I also sympathized with her and understood how she felt.

I grabbed my white linen blouse and slipped out the front door. In the east, a half moon was rising above the fringe of dark trees. A few bats were circling overhead, their sharp wings knifing through the still night air, and cicadas were singing their urgent chorus, pressing into the silence with vigor. I walked down the driveway and observed how the moon illuminated the sand, making it appear grayish-white, and slicked the green bayberry bushes with lunar shine. Although I was tired and achy and desperately wanted to lie down, Stephen needed time to explain his plan to Nathan, so that upon my return, they would have talked through and resolved everything. Yet, as I contemplated Stephen's strange suggestion, I became more uneasy. Nathan wouldn't be comfortable dividing Stephen with me, even if nothing sexual occurred—and it wouldn't. As for my own feelings for Stephen, could I vanquish them? The separation between emotional intimacy and lovemaking was thin, and considering how recently we had been involved, temptations lingered, at least on my side. My sexual attraction to Stephen also circuitously connected me to Nathan, descending into troublesome territory. Mulling over this problematic arrangement, my determination to sever the physical closeness with Stephen solidified, despite how much I was drawn to him and prized the caring that we shared, the attentions I was unlikely to ever receive again.

"You can't hurt Nathan," I admonished myself.

My son had always been my foremost concern. This time, however, my age-old priorities weren't so simple to follow, yet it would be wrong to place Nathan in an untenable position, leaving him to speculate about what was happening behind my closed door. As much as I hated the idea of sleeping alone, of ending the special moments with Stephen, I would.

I walked around the street and then stopped at the bottom of the driveway. Facing its rutted track, I sat on a section of split-rail fence devoid of roses, curled my arm around the post, and remembered how I used to sit astride such a fence—a three-rail fence—in my childhood. I'd attach a laundry line around the post and pretend I was riding a powerful white horse, about to gallop into an adventure. My imagination had always been fertile, providing a wealth of plots so that I could forget my loneliness—and there were long stretches of those friendless periods when classmates were busy, my mother was seeing patients, and my father was gone: first at work, then when confined to the hospital, and, later, after his death. But, tonight, the fence was not a horse who could carry me away, and I was not a girl who could escape into a fantastic adventure. I was a woman dying of cancer. Soon, I would be trapped in my own mind and body, taking a last voyage alone, whether Nathan or Hugh sat beside my bed or not.

The evening dew gathered around my shoulders like a cold shawl and I shivered. I thought about the purpose of my visit: to sort out my relationship with Hugh and to steel myself for the stressful future that lay ahead. While I'd accomplished the former, I had done little to face my personal fears and demons. Initially, Stephen had been a diversion—a lovely one—and then Nathan's admission about his life had jolted me, creating a complication that I was ill-prepared to deal with now. In addition, my disillusionment with Nathan—his secretiveness and deceit—was a severe shock that would require time to overcome. Time I might not have.

"Mom?" Nathan was trotting down the driveway. "I was getting worried," he said, approaching.

"It's a nice night. I needed to walk a little to settle dinner."

Nathan grabbed the fence's top rail and leaned forward. "Okay." After inhaling some air, he added, "I wanted to check that you weren't upset, Mom. About my being gay."

"No, I'm not. I just didn't anticipate your revelation—that part was distressing—that I hadn't known. But I'm fine with you being gay."

"All right. That's a relief. And as for everything else? I'm sorry for the things I said."

"I am too. We'll get through this."

"Yeah, we will." He dipped his head and removed his hands from the fence. Straightening to his full height, he paused before continuing. "So, Mom, Stephen told me what the two of you discussed."

"Yes?"

The lines on his forehead deepened. "Okay, well, I ran down here to tell you that I can't accept you and Stephen carrying on in the next bedroom. It's just out of the question." He said this in a rush, like a prepared speech. "I'm sorry but that's how I feel."

"Carrying on" sounded dismissive, like he was trivializing the beautiful moments that Stephen and I had shared. His underlying presumption also irritated me because it implied that Nathan valued his needs more than mine, which was the point I'd made with him earlier.

"Nathan, it would be helpful if you could reconsider what you just said. Particularly in light of our conversation after dinner."

He gave me a blank look.

"You're not honoring how I feel about my special time with Stephen, even if it was brief." Here, I paused, allowing my inference to hover in the air between us: that his affair with Stephen was also short. "Yes, Stephen and I discussed his solution. While it's superficially fair, it doesn't resolve anything." He began to speak, but I touched his arm. "I can't continue to share a bed with him. It's not right. I can't. I won't."

In the moonlight, the healthy color of Nathan's skin was bleached to a sickly white. Dark shadows fell away from the angle of his nose, and the overhang of his brow shadowed his eyes, giving him a ghoulish appearance. I shuddered to imagine what I looked like.

"Oh," he murmured, looking away.

I gave him a chance to say more. When he didn't, I said, "I understand that you want to be with Stephen. Maybe the two of you should go to a motel in town or to Stephen's place in Boston."

He twisted his head in surprise. "What? The reason I'm here is to be with you."

"I know and I'm very grateful that you came. But this is an unusual chance. Be with Stephen, for however long you need. Come home in a few days, a week, or whenever you're ready. See if he's the person you've been searching for and let him make a decision about you."

Nathan stared upward at the moon, as if its cool light was beneficial like the sun's. For a second, he basked in relief resulting from my acquiescence, but this reaction was momentary, as, perhaps, he realized how fast he'd cast aside his commitment to me. "Are you sure?"

I nodded. "Yes, I am. Now, is there anything else you want to say?" I asked, hoping that he would confide about the results of the genetic testing.

"No. We're good, Mom."

Nathan gave me his hand to help me off the fence. After he did, I threw my arms around his shoulders and pulled him close. "I wish we had talked years ago. And that I'd helped you more with Hugh. I'm sorry."

Nathan held me tightly. "I'm sorry, too, Mom."

We disengaged and walked to the front door, hand in hand.

"Speak with Stephen about leaving and let me know what you wish to do."

—

Inside the house, we found Stephen resting on the living room sofa, a glass of wine on the coffee table beside him. He swiveled his legs to the floor, sat upright, and gave us a quizzical look.

"Stephen, could I discuss something with you for a minute?" I asked.

With a glance at Nathan, he rose and followed me down the hall into the bedroom. I closed the door and perched on the edge of the bed, though I wanted to collapse upon it instead. I was exhausted and my back pain had steadily increased all evening.

"What's up, Bess?" He took a seat next to me and placed his arm around my shoulders.

The familiarity felt uncomfortable. We couldn't pretend that everything was the same as it had been. I eased his arm away and took his hand.

"I just spoke with Nathan. As you probably know, he's not happy with you being in here with me."

"That's what he told me."

"Okay, well, I agree with him. You should be with Nathan. No half and half arrangement because he'll feel like you haven't made a clear choice. If you've made one, that is."

"I see."

I tried to interpret his expression, yet his face conveyed little. "I don't mean to decide for you or to minimize what happened between us. I felt really flattered, cared for, like I'd been given one last chance to be happy for a short while. I will always cherish our time together…"

"But?"

"But we shouldn't continue. Although you don't like labels, you're gay—or more gay than straight. You belong with someone who's right for you, someone younger and healthier, and I'm not that person. I hope Nathan is. Maybe the two of you should go somewhere…to be alone."

Stephen gazed intently at me, his eyes fixed on mine. "We can't leave, Bess. I'm sure Nathan will realize this once we've talked."

I made no reply and noted that he hadn't addressed our relationship. "And do you agree about us? We need to agree—"

"Hey, you're over-thinking this." He gave my fingers a gentle squeeze. "Everything will be fine."

"What do you mean? You've just had sex with my son, haven't you?"

Stephen dipped his head, which I took as confirmation, yet he seemed hesitant to admit this, as if I concerned him more than

Nathan. "Okay," he said. "I get your point about Nathan being a more logical choice, but there's one person you left out of your deliberations."

"Who?"

He gestured at me. "You, Bess. You forgot yourself. What you want. As usual, in the order of the three of us, you've placed yourself last. A distant last. Nathan first, me second."

"He's my son."

"And me? Why should I come next?"

"I don't know."

"Yes, you do. You believe that if you step aside, I'll be with Nathan, he'll be happy, and you won't have to worry about his future. So, in a way, it's still about your son, and, unless I'm wrong, you want the same thing for me—to find someone."

I couldn't argue with his conclusion. I nodded.

"You know what I think about this? My role is to help you be more selfish. This is the time when you're totally justified in doing as you wish, whatever it is. If not now, when? Wouldn't this be what you would advise one of your clients? If they had Stage IV pancreatic cancer? To live life to the fullest? Do whatever they wanted?" He wrapped both of his hands around mine. "And, Bess, my other role is to help Nathan be less selfish."

"Are you going to ask my son to step aside?" I shook my head. "No, he would never forgive me. I can't risk estranging Nathan more than I already have, not when we have so little time left and he's lost his job and his relationship with Melissa. What you're suggesting is too weird. I couldn't do it." My head churned with conflicting impulses. "And on top of that, I still don't understand why you're attracted to me."

Stephen ignored what I'd said. "There's an obvious solution."

He let go of my hands and embraced me again. Regardless of my protest, I succumbed to the warmth of his body. I wanted him—this part of our relationship—regardless of whether it was okay with Nathan or whether I was behaving in a sane and ethical fashion.

"Do you mean about tonight?" I whispered.

"Not exactly. I haven't spoken with Nathan about this, but he'll be fine with my idea."

I pulled a few inches away. "Go ahead."

"I must stay with you, Bess."

His tone astonished me. "Must?"

Stephen gave me a peaceful smile that transformed his face into a serene mask. Suddenly, it almost seemed that his intention to remain in my life was preordained, and he was merely playing a role, reciting lines that had been written long ago or spoken before.

"We won't be together this evening but afterward, yes. You need me. So does Nathan. We both know he's not as strong as he should be or will need to be. Not for what lies ahead."

Sadly, I agreed with Stephen's assessment. I wasn't confident that my son could handle my care on his own. He might be motivated and emotionally committed at the moment, but Nathan wasn't tough. As Stephen implied, it was valid to be afraid he would disappear when things became difficult—he'd already become distracted by Stephen and veered from his promise to focus on me.

In a level voice, I said, "Nathan will be a good caretaker." Lying was not my habit, but I fervently wished that Nathan would manage.

Stephen looked at me askance, then his expression softened into amused skepticism. He knew I wasn't being honest, that we concurred about my son. I found Stephen's insightfulness unsettling. It felt like he possessed omniscient perception and was able to fly high above Nathan and myself to view our flaws and weaknesses with precision.

"Do you accept my proposal, Bess?" he asked.

"Your proposal?" I separated from him, stood, and walked toward the window. The moon was casting long shadows from the trees, striping the sandy dunes. "So, do I have this right? You'll sleep with Nathan tonight and are thinking about returning to Stamford with us? Living in the house and continuing with him?"

"Yes. All of that. If you want. And being your main support if

Nathan panics or, as the Brits say, throws a 'wobbly.'"

I turned to face Stephen. "And what about you? You have a life in Boston…friends and work to do. Why would you want to move and into such a difficult situation?"

"I've moved a lot. That doesn't concern me."

"Is it Nathan? Are you really interested in him and that's the reason?" I asked this because Stephen's attitude toward my son seemed distant, almost mechanical.

"I like Nathan a lot."

This was not the passionate avowal of a man in love or even a man heading in that direction. Yet, if Stephen was willing to come to Stamford to be with Nathan, he must be sincerely attracted to my son. Or was he faking his attraction because of me?

I couldn't contain my incredulity. "Enough to live with him?"

Stephen chuckled. "Of course! It'll be okay. Anyway, Nathan will need some help for some other issues too. He's dealing with the news about the BRCA2 gene mutation, right?"

"Oh. Yes." I was stunned that Nathan had disclosed this to Stephen and not to me. But how did Stephen know I was aware of the test results? Nathan had no idea Melissa had broken his confidence and neither did Stephen. "Did he tell you?"

"I guessed. Had a fifty-percent chance of getting it correct."

I observed Stephen closely. He seemed untroubled by the possibility that his new lover might die prematurely, thus repeating what had happened with Terry.

"It doesn't bother you that Nathan might have cancer in the future?"

"Any of us could be in the same boat. Or have a heart attack, stroke, car accident. I don't let my anxieties stop me from living… or rather, I don't let my fear of dying stop me from living."

"A wise philosophy. Might be a little late for me to adopt." I hesitated, balancing the welcome news that Stephen would be with us against my misgivings about Stephen's odd reaction to my son.

"So what do you think?"

"I don't know. This is very sudden." I felt a host of conflicted feelings, beginning with my disappointment in Nathan and concluding with my health, the abrupt end to every contemplation. "I suppose this is a good solution," I said, tentatively. "I was planning to leave once I heard from Hugh about the divorce…whether he'll vacate the house without a fight."

"That's fine. I'm ready whenever you are."

Stephen seemed oddly casual, as if we were college kids about to go on a carefree lark. I didn't know whether to be pleased or worried, but in either case, this choice was the only viable one if Stephen was firm in his commitment to one or both of us. "The house has four bedrooms, one of which I use for an office. It has a desk, filing cabinets, and a bed. You can work there."

"It wouldn't be an inconvenience?"

I shook my head.

"That sounds perfect. Thank you," he replied. "Now, Bess, please come here."

I walked toward him but kept a little space between us. "Stephen, you'll need to ask Nathan if he's okay with your plan. Unless I'm wildly off base, I think he really likes you and wants a relationship. A serious one."

He laughed. "Don't worry. Nathan will be thrilled with my suggestion. Ever since he saw me at the bar—"

"The bar?"

"Yeah. Remember I said that I'd seen Nathan before? I was kind of teasing him, to see how he would respond. Anyhow, we were both in a gay bar in town. Three nights ago."

"I thought Nathan arrived the night before he came here. It was too late so he stayed at a motel—that's what he told me."

"No, Bess, he didn't. Nathan spent that night and the following day and night in Provincetown. Besides, the last ferry docks at seven o'clock, and even if there is a special August ferry, that comes by eight."

"Which means what he said was untrue." For all of Nathan's avowals of "being there" for me, he had placed his social life first and had also lied about it.

Stephen frowned, guessing that this news had disturbed me. "Nothing happened at the bar. He didn't come over and talk or anything. Only checked me out from across the room. But it was obvious that he was interested."

"Why didn't you speak to him?"

"I don't know." Stephen shrugged. "He's an attractive guy. It just wasn't the right time."

"The right time?"

"Yeah. I left a few minutes later, but if I hadn't, Nathan would have made a move. One way or the other, I expected he would find me. Provincetown is a pretty small place."

Was that why Nathan had postponed his arrival? To search for Stephen on the beach and to spend more time at gay clubs? Or to get a little tan, which I'd noticed when he first came?

"Was Nathan talking or dancing with anyone?"

"No, not while I was there."

Stephen didn't say if he himself had met a man and decamped to a motel room, and I didn't ask. It was none of my business, nor did I wish to hear the answer.

"Well, we've left Nathan for a long while—he'll wonder what's happening." I rose to my feet. "Oh, and please don't mention to Nathan I know about the BRCA2 results. He'll tell me when he's ready." I gave him a quick kiss. "I'll go say goodnight while you move your things into the guest room."

—

In the living room, Nathan was peering through the large windows. When I entered, he glanced at me. "Everything okay?"

"Yes. Stephen is sleeping with you. He's removing his clothes from my room."

"So it's done? The...relationship?"

"Yes. He can explain what he wants to do next. All I ask is that you be certain of your own wishes and consider everything with deliberation and care. Will you please do that?"

"I will." He laughed. "I'm not a kid anymore, Mom."

"No, you aren't. But remember that you've just met Stephen. Sometimes chemistry overpowers judgment. Believe me, I know."

Nathan smiled at this. I could see he was overjoyed with my decision and trying to contain his happiness in respect for my loss. "Okay, I promise to be careful."

I doubted he would be prudent or cautious. Nathan was as be-dazzled by Stephen as I had been and still was, though perhaps I'd regained some balance. I nodded, walked into the kitchen, filled the kettle for the morning coffee, and poured a glass of water to take to my room. On my way back, I stopped beside Nathan, who was still standing by the window.

"Thank you for telling me about being gay. I'm glad you did."

"I'm glad, too, Mom. Thanks for being so understanding. But you always are. I should have known that and not waited so long."

"We're good, then?"

"Yeah."

"You can always come to me." As I uttered these words, ones I'd said many times before to my son, I knew this promise wasn't an indefinite one. Nathan's face fell, as he also realized this. I kissed him on the cheek. "Now, I'm not feeling great so I'm going to bed. Good night, dear."

By the time I returned to the bedroom, Stephen had cleared the closet of his possessions, though the fragrance of his aftershave lingered in the air. I closed the door and half-wished Nathan had never come to visit. This thought—no more than a flash—filled me with disgust. I had become a woman I didn't recognize. It was as if the pernicious effects of the cancer were destroying the self I'd worked so hard to create during hours of therapy with a su-pervising counselor and over years of conscientious self-analysis.

After changing into a nightgown, I crawled into bed, missing Stephen.

17

When I awoke a few minutes before nine o'clock the next morning, the pain was terrible. The second fentanyl patch wasn't due to be changed for another day, so the dose should still be effective, and both patches were tight. Slowly, I lifted my feet from under the covers and placed them on the floor. My back hurt in the usual location, the ache spreading to my shoulders, but the area was wider and more intense, plus there was a new pain at the upper right of my abdomen and in the center. Had the tumors enlarged overnight? I wrapped my arms around my stomach and rocked forward, trying to relieve the pressure.

This did no good. Hoping a hot shower might help, I tried that and felt slightly better but not much. The pain made hooking my bra difficult, but I succeeded after a few attempts, and then dressed in loose jeans and a navy blouse. After giving into my exhaustion for a moment, I made the bed and checked my phone. Hugh had left four messages. The divorce letter had been delivered. At first, he expressed alarm that I'd lost my mind. The second message attempted to cajole me by saying how ill I was and how much I needed him. The third and fourth messages regressed to incredulity and then sped forward into outrage. At the end of each recording, he beseeched me to return his calls. I turned off the phone.

Nathan and Stephen were in the kitchen. I took a deep breath and went to join them.

"Good morning, Mom," Nathan said. He was sitting at the table, facing in my direction. His eyes looked red and tired, but he gave me a big grin, which confirmed all I needed to know about the state of his romance with Stephen.

"Good morning," I replied.

Stephen rose and hugged me, though he did so with care. "Did you sleep well?"

I gazed at him without speaking. In those few seconds, his blue eyes clouded. He saw how I felt.

"Yes. Sorry to have overslept."

"That's not like you." Nathan sipped some coffee and ate the last bite of his toast.

"What would you like for breakfast, Bess?" Stephen asked.

My appetite was minus zero. "A scrambled egg?"

"I could make some sausage," Nathan suggested.

"Probably a little too much," Stephen told him.

"But you love sausage, don't you?"

"Yes. Not today." I poured half a cup of coffee and tried to stifle the image of fat-oozing meat.

—

After I ate half of my egg and drank a little coffee and orange juice, I immediately regretted it. I sat in my chair, praying that my stomach would settle. While I considered a fast trip to the bathroom, Nathan asked if I wanted to go whale watching. Being on a tossing boat was the furthest thing from what I wished to do. Politely, I said no, all the while wondering if sex had frazzled Nathan's brain. His lack of sensitivity was appalling.

Stephen, perhaps seeing my queasy expression, stepped in. "I don't think your mother is up for anything that requires much exertion."

Nathan examined me as if for the first time all morning. "Oh, yeah. Sorry, Mom."

"You two can go," I replied, half hoping they would. On the other hand, I was anxious about how I was feeling and not altogether sure I should be left alone.

"Maybe another time," Stephen suggested. "We'll figure out something to do."

I appreciated how gracefully he had steered the discussion away from my physical condition. I mustered a weak smile and brought my few dishes to the sink. "Now, I hate to mention it, but Hugh received my letter about the divorce and he's not happy. I need to speak with him, to be sure he's agreed to my requests."

I left the table, shut the bedroom door, and sat quietly until the nausea passed. After I detached my cell phone from its charger, I tried to steady my nerves before dialing Hugh's number.

———

"Bess? Is that you?" Hugh's confident voice sounded frail.

"Yes. I received your phone messages. And I presume you received the letter from my attorney?"

"From George?" He let out a lengthy sigh. "I don't understand this at all. Why are you doing this now? After all of our years together."

"Because of all of our years together. I've had enough, Hugh. I realize this is upsetting, to move out of the house—"

"That's not the main thing," he cut in. "I love you, Bess! You know that! What would I do without you?" He paused, then added, "And what will you do without me?"

"You'll manage," I said quietly. The order with which he had listed our situations was indicative of his true priorities. As usual, Hugh couldn't perceive the effect of his words, of his me-first selfishness that I'd also just witnessed in Nathan.

"But you can't be alone."

"Nathan is coming home to stay with me for a while. In fact, he's here now. He came because he wanted us to spend time together." I didn't mention Stephen, nor did I address Hugh's question concerning how he would carry on alone.

"What? Did you invite him?"

I could hear that Hugh felt excluded and hurt. "No, I didn't."

He said nothing for a moment. "But what about his job? He's always telling us that he's too busy to visit."

"Nathan is working everything out."

Hugh sputtered, spouting logistical issues about the separation that were reasonable but not persuasive. I sat on the bed, feeling miserable, but my husband needed a chance to list his objections and to know that I'd heard him clearly. To accomplish that, I mirrored his statements, a technique of my trade, which I regretted doing. These perfunctory responses should have been obvious to Hugh, but he was too upset to notice.

Finally, he made a heartfelt admission. "Bess, I know I haven't been the best husband, the most faithful husband. That I've disappointed you many times. If I had been you, I would have left me years ago and started a new life with someone else. You deserved better. The only thing I can say is that I do love you, have always loved you since the night we met. Do you remember it? During the summer production of the opera. What was it called?"

"*The Tales of Hoffmann.* I was singing Nicklausse. The trouser role."

"Yes. You were so beautiful and sang so brilliantly."

The single staged performance of my short career. Now, reminded of the part I'd played, I smiled at the irony. Nicklausse was Hoffmann's companion in his amatory adventures, watching as Hoffmann falls in love with one woman after another, none of the choices appropriate or rational. Despite witnessing Hoffmann's folly, Nicklausse is loyal to the end.

"A very prophetic beginning," I replied, "considering the part and the plot."

Hugh fell silent as he digested the significance of what I'd said. "I never thought about that, Bess, but you're right. I've been a fool, and I've treated you very badly." The apology was almost a whisper. "Is there nothing I can say or do to change your mind?"

"I appreciate how you feel, Hugh, but we've traveled down the same path for years. You say you're sorry, I forgive you, and the drama begins again. I don't want to continue. I can't."

Hugh didn't respond at first. Perhaps he realized that I was beyond persuasion. "So it's over." This was a statement, not a question.

"Yes, it's over."

He sighed. "And you want me to leave the house?"

"I do. To begin the formal separation."

Once again, he said nothing. I heard the leather of his armchair creak as Hugh sat down. Although he liked to roam in relationships and enjoyed spontaneity within them—except with me—Hugh was a man of order and constancy at home and at work. He read the morning paper each day at eight o'clock in the sunroom, sitting in his favorite chair by the window; beside him, a mug of coffee. Always coffee with cream and two sugars, never tea. Tea was for the afternoon when he returned from the university. During the school year, he rotated his Oxford shirts, striped ties, and tweed jackets, beginning on Monday. Upsetting all that was familiar and regular in his life would be traumatic and was a great deal to ask of Hugh.

"Bess, I've lived here for thirty-seven years! This is my home. Our home. I thought we'd live out our last days here." He hesitated, obviously struck by the poignancy of his remark. "Where will I go?"

Of course, Hugh could return after I died, depending on how he and Nathan eventually resolved ownership of the house. "Why don't you rent a place from Lewis?" I suggested. "Doesn't he have a two-bedroom apartment available downtown? One of his investment properties?"

"Yes, I think he does."

His fast response indicated that he'd already contemplated this possibility. "Well, then, give him a call."

"How can I move all my things? My desk and reading chair? My books and papers?"

Hugh was not in the best shape and shouldn't lift boxes. "Just take your clothes and some personal items. You can get the rest later," I replied. "And maybe hire one of your students."

"What about Nathan?" he asked. "If he's coming to live with you, why can't he help?"

He had a good point, yet I could picture my son's face if the idea was proposed to him. He would be less than thrilled to be alone with Hugh and not delighted to leave Stephen. "You could ask him."

"No. Better coming from you."

I was hesitant to do so but consented to speak to Nathan because I felt too sick to argue. After that, Hugh softened his tone, perhaps because he missed his son and was eager to spend time with him—they hadn't seen each other since Easter. I found it heartbreaking that Hugh didn't realize how seriously he had alienated Nathan, though he was aware of the discord and had mentioned it to me when Nathan failed to come home for a birthday celebration or a holiday. However, like so much I was learning about my son, even I hadn't fully discerned the depth of Nathan's bitterness toward his father until our recent conversations. I considered divulging this to Hugh, but Nathan's anger was entangled with his homosexuality, and I had no right to reveal that confidence.

We spoke for a while longer, discussing possessions that were his versus things that were mine. At the end, Hugh promised to leave two days from now, by mid afternoon, if he could. I had been planning to drive back to Stamford then and hoped he would abide by the schedule.

As we said goodbye, I felt very depressed. The transition would be difficult for Hugh even if he could find a replacement in his bed—not that we had shared one recently—as well as for me. I would miss his optimism, humor, and intelligent perceptions about politics and world events; the pleasure of his companionship in the simple activities of daily life. Regardless of our interpersonal conflicts, our history was long and complex. In many ways, we had grown into each other, for better or for worse, and cleaving us apart would be a shock to both of us. I was also concerned that Hugh was counting on Nathan to compensate for my absence and would be gravely disappointed if his son didn't make the effort, which very well could happen.

With a sad heart, I disconnected and fought the temptation to do what I always do—accept Hugh's remorse and continue with him until the next problem arose. This time, his regret sounded sincere, his sorrow profound, his love genuine. I could feel the difference. But it was too late.

I waited by the phone, expecting Hugh to call again and present a fresh case as to why we shouldn't separate. He didn't. The silence in the room magnified the soft chatter of the birds outside, but I couldn't concentrate on their songs or absorb their joyfulness. Instead, I succumbed to dejection, realizing how much I had just lost and how little happiness lay in the future.

"Stay positive, Bess," I whispered. "And be grateful." For my dear friend Susan; for Nathan, whose presence over the next months would hopefully be a loving one; and for Stephen, who was an unexpected gift.

I reached for my phone and turned it off. In doing so, it suddenly occurred to me that I'd never seen Stephen use a cell phone, which was peculiar. All younger men were glued to their devices, yet I couldn't recall him holding a tablet, phone, or laptop. If Stephen was running a freelance insurance business, he would be obligated to check in regularly in case clients had made inquiries or claims, even while he was on vacation. No one went off-line these days, especially not a man who worked for himself. Probably the phone was in his car, and he'd made calls from there.

I came to my feet, though it was difficult to straighten my posture. My abdomen ached and felt swollen, almost distended. Should I take an oxycodone? Within certain guidelines, Dr. Melbourne had given me latitude to adjust the mixture and dose if the pain worsened. I decided to delay the pill in the hope that walking around the house would ease the discomfort. Forcing myself to stand upright, I left the bedroom and wandered through the living room and kitchen into the studio, where I found Nathan and Stephen. A sketchbook was resting on Stephen's knees, and he was drawing my son. Apparently, he had shown Nathan the portrait of me because it was lying on the table.

"Wow, what a fine likeness!" I exclaimed, looking over Stephen's shoulder.

"I thought I'd make a pair." He glanced at me and smiled.

I knew he was doing this for Nathan, so he could have pictures of both of us to commemorate our time together here. This thoughtfulness touched my heart. I laid my hand on Stephen's shoulder, leaned close to his ear, and whispered, "Thank you."

—

I had no idea what the two men planned to do after lunch, but I needed to talk with my son about Hugh. I made turkey sandwiches with cranberry sauce, sprigs of basil from the garden, and slices of Brie. I couldn't eat anything but sat with the two of them on the patio.

"Nathan, as you know, I spoke with your father earlier. He's rather upset."

"I bet he is."

"He really is," I emphasized, wishing Nathan would evince some kindness toward Hugh. When my son made no reply, I continued. "Well, though you don't have much sympathy for him, he's almost seventy. With his high blood pressure, moving boxes and furniture isn't a smart idea. I suggested that he hire someone, but he hoped you might come and help."

Nathan began to protest. I leaned over and touched his cheek. "I'll be home in two days, which is when Hugh will be out of the house. If you would drive to Stamford this afternoon and assist him tomorrow and the following morning, I'm sure he would greatly appreciate it."

He backed away. "But, Mom, why should I?"

I folded my hands in my lap. "Nathan, he's your father and he needs you. And so do I. If you could do this, Hugh is less likely to try a last minute protest. It would be an enormous relief for you to sort him out and to call me after Hugh has left. If you're willing, you can take my car."

Nathan crossed his arms. "I don't know."

"I understand you don't want to leave Stephen, but it's not for long. Besides, you came here for me, didn't you? Well, you can help me the most by doing this large favor. It's also important that you speak with Hugh about your job and about Melissa. If you want to tell him you're gay, that's your choice." I moved closer to Nathan. "Will you do this, please?"

He compressed his mouth, showing signs of resistance. Stephen noticed Nathan's reaction, stood, walked around the table, and placed a hand on his shoulder.

"Come on. You go home and make everything right with your dad. That's important. Show him you're concerned about him and clear the air. When I get there, after a while and depending how your conversation goes, we can take him out to dinner and tell him about us. If you want to do that, I mean. But working on your relationship now will make it a lot easier later. How about it, Nathan?"

Nathan gave us each an aggrieved look, like we were ganging up on him. Slowly, he nodded his acquiescence.

"Good guy!" Stephen exclaimed, wrapping his hands around Nathan's head and pulling him against his chest.

After the two separated, I faced Stephen. "And, if it's agreeable with you, we could return to Stamford in your car—maybe stopping in Boston for more of your things."

He let go of Nathan and tousled his hair. "Bess, I'm happy to drive you home. It will be my pleasure."

—

The two men disappeared into the guest room. I called Hugh to inform him of Nathan's arrival tonight, suggesting that he cook a nice dinner. Regardless of Hugh's dismay about the divorce, he was delighted with the news. After we said goodbye, I wrote a check to Nathan for $5,000 from my brokerage account. Because of his job loss, he might need some money. In the studio, I found sheets of cardboard to protect the two pencil drawings Stephen had done.

About fifteen minutes later, Stephen and Nathan carried Nathan's duffel bag, raincoat, and briefcase to my car. I followed them outside and watched my son. He was almost handsome enough to be with Stephen, though no one was in Stephen's class. Nathan's hair sparkled like metallic bronze, and, as he turned toward me, his brown eyes caught the light. Compared with Stephen's substantial, muscular physique, Nathan was slim and moved more gracefully, with a lightness in his step befitting a lifelong runner. His features, his build were similar to my own, which pleased me, but then, too, he'd inherited my BRCA2 gene, which was frightening. How devastating to know I wouldn't be alive to care for Nathan if he became ill! And what a tragedy to know the possible future and yet not to possess one myself. I was also sorry that he hadn't mentioned the genetic testing. Had he avoided the issue to shield me from additional stress or to shield himself, so he could preserve a state of denial about the results?

Stephen gave Nathan a huge hug, who in turn initiated a sultry kiss. While I was glad the two men were comfortable showing affection in front of me, I mused over the paradox of our awkward arrangement: if I had given Stephen such a hug and sexy kiss, my son would have been outraged. I erased this thought from my mind and walked over to Nathan. He smiled and folded me in his arms.

"I'll see you soon, Mom. Take care."

He began to disengage, but I held him tightly, taking in his familiar scent that had changed little since his childhood. "You know how much I love you, Nathan," I whispered. "Please know that and remember."

He drew away and gave me a searching look, one that I returned. Although each parting over the last thirty months had been sad for both of us—as if we might not see each other again— this time felt especially poignant. I memorized Nathan's beautiful eyes, so like my father's, and his narrow face, so like my own, and absorbed his love and concern, which I hoped he could also see in my expression.

"Drive safely," I said, kissing his cheek. "And here. To pay for gas and whatever else." I tucked sixty dollars and the check in the breast pocket of his shirt and handed him the two portraits.

18

Stephen and I returned to the house after the BMW rounded the driveway's curve and disappeared from sight. Inside the living room, the sun was pouring through the two skylights, throwing large rectangles of light on the furniture and across the wide floorboards. Despite the joyful brightness of the room, I felt dejected because of Nathan's departure, as if it signaled more than a two-day separation. I tried to reason myself out of this foreboding, but its jaws were firmly clenched on my spirit. Was this feeling amplified because of the pain? The ache was unrelenting and becoming more intense as the hours passed.

While Stephen locked the front door, I stood beside the dining table, thinking it was noteworthy that I'd chosen to remain with a stranger rather than with my son. I wondered about Stephen, this kindly man whose history seemed hidden behind a veil. What did I really know about him? Had he truly attended Cornell? Was he an orphan who had lived in multiple homes? Did he own or rent a condo in Boston? And had he been married to a man named Terry? Stephen wore no wedding band, but neither did Hugh. Even Stephen's white car appeared to be a generic rental. So many questions I wished answered, yet how could I ask Stephen about them without sounding suspicious about the details he'd already recounted? This was the man my son was falling for or already had. Not to mention that I was also attracted to him. I should trust

Stephen, I told myself firmly.

"I imagine you're sorry to see Nathan go," Stephen said, settling in one of the armchairs.

Exhausted, I sank into the chair on the opposite side of the coffee table. "I am. I haven't seen him much. He's been busy with his job and with Melissa. But mostly he doesn't visit because of Hugh. Nathan has come a few times on my chemo days, but otherwise…"

"Otherwise, not often."

I knew what Stephen was saying: that Nathan wasn't reliable. More or less, Stephen and I had been down this stretch of road before. While I recognized that Stephen's implication was accurate, I also felt unsettled that Stephen would denigrate my son, his lover. Even if Stephen was aligning with my point of view, expressing his concern for my well-being, I was caught on the disloyalty. Once again, I questioned the nature of his feelings toward Nathan and toward me, and how he could move from one bed to another so swiftly without exhibiting any inner turmoil—or none that was visible.

"Nathan has had a difficult time lately," I said.

Stephen acknowledged this with a dip of his head. "I know."

We stared at each other. Though I sensed some awkwardness, he smiled and maintained his usual imperturbable manner.

"Shall I pick up something for dinner? I know you're not feeling like eating much."

"No, I'm not. Whatever you want is fine, Stephen."

"Okay. Nothing heavy, I promise. Do you want to come with me?"

I didn't feel like it but said I would.

—

Stephen went inside the store while I remained in the car with the windows open. I leaned an elbow against the door frame and compared how wretched I was now with how I'd felt yesterday and decided I was immeasurably worse. During the weeks off from chemo, I'd been doing fairly well except for bouts of constipation, lightheadedness, fatigue, and achiness. These new physical changes were distressing and ominous. To distract myself from my glum thoughts, I tried to open the glove compartment to see if it contained any more information about Stephen, but it was locked. Other than some sand on the floor mats, the car was bare—no cell phone or briefcase in sight. A fake pine smell permeated the interior, but since Stephen didn't seem the type to use an air freshener, this confirmed that the car was probably a rental.

When Stephen returned with a bag of groceries, he placed it in the back and squeezed into the front seat, which was tight for a man his size.

"You could have rented a bigger car," I suggested.

He glanced at me. "Yeah, next time." Throwing the transmission in reverse, he eased out of the parking space and headed for the cottage. "I need one where the steering wheel isn't stuck in my chest." He chuckled at this.

"I hope it won't be a problem to drive to Stamford. How long have you reserved the car?"

"For a month…or less, depending."

"Depending on what?"

"Oh, I don't know. Where I am. What I'm doing."

Stephen didn't elaborate further. He drove carefully but fast, much as I did. By the time we arrived, I was relieved to be stationary because my stomach had been sloshing around dangerously—the last mile on the bumpy road had been especially taxing. Upon entering the house, I collapsed on the sofa.

"Doesn't seem like you're doing so well, Bess."

I looked at him standing in front of me, holding the grocery bag. "I feel pretty terrible."

"Hmm. Well, why don't you lie down while I put the food away. I thought some chicken and white rice might work for tonight. With some baked beans."

At the mention of the beans, I made a face.

Stephen laughed. "Only kidding about the beans. Bland. That's what you'll get."

I shook my head, rose from the couch, and walked into the bedroom. After removing my shoes, I slipped under the sheets, circled my stomach with my arms, and tried to sleep.

I couldn't. I retrieved my cosmetics case, rooted inside for the bottle of oxycodone, took one tablet, and returned to bed. As I experimented with various positions, none providing any respite, I thought about that first night after receiving the cancer prognosis from the gastroenterologist. Because I was upset, Hugh had slept with me, but, as usual, he had fallen asleep in minutes. I remember staring out the window at the black sky, and slowly a sensation of relief had spread over me. Ever since my mid-fifties, checking the obituaries in the newspapers had become a daily activity. Whenever I read about someone my age or younger who had died, I felt a flash of panic about my own eventual mortality. This anxiety had continued to smolder for years: When would my life end? From what disease or accident? And what would my circumstances be then? Well, suddenly, once the Stage IV diagnosis had been confirmed, the unknown time was whittled down to months, the cause was certain—barring the unexpected—and only my situation needed clarification, which had ultimately provoked this journey to Cape Cod. Yes, I had been very afraid that night, but I had also experienced a strange comfort, a kind of liberation, knowing that my future had been switched from infinite to finite, from ambiguous to clear, and that I had little ability to alter my fate. Death was on my agenda, written in black indelible ink.

—

Stephen woke me two hours later. I wished he hadn't because the abdominal pain was worse. I moaned and rolled over to look at him.

His eyes widened and then an expression of sorrow passed over his face. In a strangely even tone, he said, "Bess, you need to look at yourself in the mirror."

"What? Why?"

He helped me stand. My head ached. I was shaky and hot,

like a fever had set in. With Stephen supporting my elbow, we walked into the bathroom, where he switched on the light. The dazzling white tiles and the harsh brightness made me half-cover my eyes. I lowered my hand from my face, took a few more steps, and confronted the mirror.

"Oh, my god!" Shocked, I inhaled sharply.

19

"It can't be! Jaundice!" My face and the whites of my eyes were a pale, sickening yellow. I stared at my image, horrified, fell back against Stephen's chest, and raised my fingers to my cheek, feeling like it belonged to someone else. "Oh, Stephen," I whispered, "I know what this means."

He placed his arms around me. "So do I, Bess."

"When did this happen?"

"A few hours ago. Didn't you notice the change?"

"No. I just felt really awful."

Had Stephen seen the alteration in my skin color earlier and not told me? Why not? Confused by his composed demeanor, I scrutinized him in the mirror, but his expression revealed only calm concern.

I spun around and grasped his arms tightly. "This is really serious. I think the tumors have grown into the bile duct."

"That sounds likely," he agreed. "I guess the bile duct will need to be surgically cleared. An ERCP."

Why was Stephen familiar with such a specific technique—an endoscopic procedure? He hadn't even finished his undergraduate pre-med degree. "How do you know about that?"

"I pick up things here and there."

While an ERCP might open the duct, it might not work, either, in which case an interventional radiologist would need to fish through the liver, from above the obstruction. Shortly after my diagnosis, I'd plunged into research about pancreatic cancer and had also spoken with a friend in California, a retired surgeon, and pressed him to list the issues that might eventually arise—one he mentioned was the bile duct. Another possibility was the impingement of the tumors on the celiac ganglia, a juncture of nerves near the head of the pancreas, where my primary tumors were located. Considering the new centralized pain I was experiencing, it was likely this complication was occurring. Although a block on these nerves could be surgically done, it was one more procedure to add to the others. My friend had counseled me not to think about any of these problems, but of course I had. And always of the opinion that knowledge was superior to ignorance, I'd read about all three operations as well as the partial splenectomy.

I explained these details to Stephen. "Even if the ERCP is successful, the cancer is still present." This admission suddenly struck me hard, and I was barely able to speak. "And obviously metastasizing again."

"No surgery to remove the tumors is possible, right?"

I shook my head and managed to say that a Whipple Procedure couldn't be done—even at the beginning—because the tumors were spread throughout the liver. And then, although I knew I was coming across as unhinged, I began describing all the other actions that might be required to keep me alive, which turned into a spew about test results, chemo drugs, painkillers—all laced with medical jargon, words and phrases that I had memorized as if they could act as talismans to ward off my deepest fears. My voice rose and thinned as my agitation increased. Finally, I stopped, exhausted by my outburst.

Stephen was watching me carefully and nodding, as if he already knew this information. Because he hadn't related having any friends with pancreatic cancer, what was the source of his detailed knowledge?

"It doesn't sound good, does it?" he asked.

I swallowed, trying to slow the surge of panic that had overtaken me. "It sounds like the start of the end." The weight of my words made my knees weaken. I held onto Stephen, afraid I might collapse. "Perhaps in a few months. Or…less."

"Yes."

"With weeks in the hospital," I added. "With the morphine levels being raised until I can't think straight."

"Would they try chemo again?"

I exhaled an unsteady breath and summoned my professional self, the woman who had made a career of remaining composed during crises. "Maybe, but I have a problem with a fluctuating platelet count. After one or two infusions, we might have to stop and do a partial splenectomy. To release platelets from the spleen so we can continue. Or the chemo won't work any longer, and the second type won't be effective, either." My momentary control evaporated. I felt dizzy, almost weightless, as if I had spiraled out of myself. I looked up at Stephen. His eyes were filled with sadness. "And the bile duct requires immediate surgery."

He acknowledged this truth and was silent. We stood, staring at each other. The faint buzzing sound from the lights by the bathroom mirror filled my ears with white noise. A minute passed and then Stephen touched my forehead.

"Bess, I'm sorry, but I think you also have a fever." He sighed, stepped away from me, and opened the medicine cabinet. After checking several bottles, he found some aspirin. "Here, take these and then let's lie down for a few minutes."

I swallowed two aspirins and risked a last look in the mirror. Once again, I was alarmed by the abnormal color of my skin. I resembled some kind of alien being. This wasn't me. Not Elizabeth Lynch. Dazed, I staggered out of the bathroom to the bed, where I lay next to Stephen. He extended his arm under my neck, enfolded my shoulders, and gently placed my head under his chin. I thought about Nathan and my resolve to cease all physical closeness with Stephen, but I was helpless to separate from him. For a long while, neither of us spoke. Although a flood of tears might fall later, at the moment I was too stunned to cry. I recalled the journal accounts of several end-stage pancreatic cancer patients and shuddered to imagine the tortuous road ahead—for me and for Nathan, who would be forced to sit in a chair by my bedside, watching my daily disintegration, as I had watched both my parents during their last weeks. First, the pain would increase as the doctors struggled to keep pace with it. My bowels would continually block due to the morphine. Then, slowly, I would weaken and be unable to walk. A catheter would be inserted, and, at some point, solid food would be replaced with soft food until I couldn't manage that. Toward the end, swallowing fluids would be impossible.

Death would follow several days later, when I would be in hospice, on the cancer wing of the hospital, or at home. The progression would be relentless, a horrendous march that would tax Nathan terribly and would reduce me to a body that bore no resemblance to the one I had always inhabited. Jaundice was one of the first visible signs of this sequence, but as the cancer ate through my pancreas, liver, and other organs—as the morphine was increased—my mind and personality would disintegrate. I feared this far more than pain.

I shared these thoughts with Stephen, who listened mostly without speaking, except to indicate agreement with my assessment. As I considered this bleak future, it occurred to me that he hadn't recommended we rush to the hospital, despite the medical emergency, nor had he offered to drive me to Stamford, to my doctor. Instead, Stephen had been caring and steady, without directing any course of action. Had he anticipated the jaundice and the increase in pain? If so, by what psychic divination had he foreseen these events?

"Stephen, do you think I should go home? Or to a hospital?"

He paused before responding. "What do you want to do, Bess?"

I didn't have an answer. It seemed that if I went to Stamford, everything would tumble downward like so many dominoes in a chain reaction. "If I did, I might become too incapacitated to control what occurs afterward, to decide when to stop treatment or additional interventions. My friend Susan is listed as my primary person on my health proxy, with Nathan second. I trust her absolutely, but with the university starting and her mother at home, it would be a terrific strain for Susan to be at the hospital for long hours."

"Which leaves Nathan."

"I know. And after what I've just witnessed, I'm not sure he will work well with Susan or allow her to be in charge, if she's able. And he might fight to keep me alive, even though I signed a 'do not resuscitate' order."

"But if Nathan tries to override it, he would create chaos and a legal mess."

"Yes, or he might—"

"Disappear? And not help at all?"

I sighed, reluctant to admit this possibility. "If I don't go to the hospital, what's next?"

Stephen created a small space between us. In the weak afternoon light, his eyes had lost their blueness. "Are you asking what will happen or what you should do?"

"I know what will happen. Liver and kidney failure. Toxicity, ascites, confusion, difficulty breathing, pain, coma, and death. Or, if I'm lucky, my heart will stop."

Stephen didn't refute my list. "Are you afraid?"

"Yes, I'm afraid." I sighed. "I'm also afraid for Nathan."

"And about Nathan?"

I nodded. "As for what I should do…well, I don't wish to put him through this ordeal. And I don't wish to be disappointed in him, either. To know he failed me," I whispered. "It would be unbearable for that to be my last impression of my son." I considered for a moment and conceded that Stephen was right to be worried. "Nathan might run when I need him most."

"He might."

I heard the doubt coloring his voice. While Stephen had promised to come to Stamford, in part to be with Nathan, was my son the main reason for his willingness to move from Boston? And if we didn't go to Stamford? Could I ask him to relinquish time with Nathan and to remain in Truro? It was a lot to expect of someone, to willingly stay in this stressful situation, even someone close. Unless he volunteered, it wasn't fair to put Stephen on the spot.

"You're wondering about my relationship with Nathan," Stephen said, demonstrating prescience once again. "How committed I am to him."

"Yes."

"And whether I'll continue with him after—"

"Will you?"

Stephen didn't answer at first. He ran his fingers over my hair, as if to comfort me, but also to bide time before responding. "He isn't ready. Not yet."

This inscrutable answer confused me. I concentrated hard, trying to still the mental turmoil caused by the medication, fever, and pain. Then everything clicked into place like a neat jigsaw puzzle and made sense.

"You were with Nathan only because I'm dying. To give him an incentive to be with me."

"Because it's your time, yes."

I stared at him. "And if and when he becomes ill?"

"Then I'll find Nathan wherever he is. Don't worry about that."

"But how?"

Stephen was silent.

I drew farther away from him. Who was this man beside me? I examined his pale, smooth skin; the strong neck and chest and arms; the astonishing, sculptured beauty of his face; and knew that Stephen wasn't a life insurance salesman or a guy who lived in Boston, though he might have done so for a while, during his time with Terry. Did he have a necrophiliac attraction to the dying? Or did he attach to us for some other reason?

"Who are you?" I asked, feeling a little afraid of him.

Stephen raised his eyebrows in surprise. "What do you mean, Bess?"

"Answer me!"

"Stephen Andersen." He frowned. "Are you okay? Did you take some oxycodone?"

"I did but it hasn't affected my mind."

"Are you sure?"

Maybe he was correct. I wasn't okay. Suddenly, I sensed a chilly breeze floating through the room as if spirits were gathering around us. Had Stephen summoned them or were they emanating from within him? Or was I suffering from chills produced by the fever? Yet heat seemed to be bursting through my skin, its pressure collecting behind my eyes and thudding across my forehead, like I was stuck between clashing temperatures, between two colliding fronts. And, similarly, my thoughts were crashing into each other, like cars spinning on ice. Was I losing my sanity?

"Stephen," I began, "just so I understand…you would drive me to Stamford and stay with us. At my house you would sleep with Nathan. But if I don't go, you won't return to Nathan and continue your relationship with him?"

He smiled and placed his cool cheek against my hot cheek. "Bess, I'm with you no matter what."

My doubts about why Stephen had been drawn to me resurfaced. Now they appeared in a fresh new light. I had been viewing him through the eyes of a woman, gauging his reactions to me in terms of attraction, both emotional and physical, but I was looking through the wrong lens. Our relationship had nothing to do with sex—that had only been an introductory hook, as had, possibly, his professed grief over Terry, which may have been a ploy to engage my sympathy. My gender, age, orientation, looks, or professional skills didn't matter. Stephen was interested in me because I was dying.

"Nathan really likes you, Stephen," I told him.

"I know he does. He'll find someone else, I suspect. Now that he's disclosed he's gay and has stopped trying to be straight. That's a big step forward."

"I hope you're right."

Losing Stephen and me would be an overwhelming trauma. If I went home and thus prolonged Nathan's relationship with Stephen, would it be easier for my son? Or would Stephen's departure after my death cause more pain, assuming they would have become closer during my last days? However, as much as I wanted to do the best by Nathan, I couldn't base my actions on his short-term happiness. Not any longer. I explained this to Stephen.

"I'm glad to hear that," he replied. "This time is about you. No one else."

"I've never thought that way before." I realized Stephen was repeating a previous admonition: to place myself first. I thought of all the sessions in which I'd patiently reinforced an important point to my clients, saying the same simple thing over and over until they finally heard it. I now heard Stephen's message.

"Well, you have some decisions to make," he said. "Why don't you rest? I'll make dinner." He placed the sheet over me and kissed my forehead.

After he left, I lay on my side, flipped over, and tried to sleep on my back. Regardless of my position, my abdomen was swollen and tender. If I didn't go to a hospital soon, I would quickly become sicker, and the pain would soon be unmanageable with fentanyl patches and oxycodone tablets. How long did I have before my liver failed and the pain escalated to an unbearable level? And how would Stephen handle this rapid decline alone in the house?

I was too distraught to sleep. While I was still somewhat rational, I decided to write letters to Nathan, Hugh, and Susan in case I didn't go home or something precipitous occurred. I carried my laptop to the bed and began typing, seeking to avoid melodrama and inducing guilt, especially in Nathan but also in Hugh—I saw no point in further undermining my husband. The divorce petition was sufficient chastisement. I told him to be kind and understanding with our son. To Nathan, I confessed that Melissa had shared the news about his BRCA2 genetic test. I said that I was deeply sorry about the results, that I wished I could be there to take care of him if he became ill. Melissa's intentions had been honorable, I wrote, and he shouldn't be upset with her for confiding his secret. I urged my son to find a wonderful man, an exciting new job, and to be happy and proud of himself. I hesitated about mentioning

Stephen and finally opted against it. And, similar to my entreaty to Hugh, I begged Nathan to be considerate and try his best to heal the strained relationship with his father. In Susan's note, I sent my heartfelt gratitude to her for being my most cherished friend and my best wishes to her mother and Lewis.

I labored on these for some time and left them stored as a Word document, which I could copy and paste into individual emails. Although I hesitated to do so, I also scrubbed all of my patients' records and professional files. Having completed those sad tasks, I turned off the laptop and faced the windows. It was time to deal with the far more difficult challenge of forging a course of action. If I returned home, I knew what would occur at first, with the unknown factors being what procedures would be performed in the hospital, how long I'd be there, and how much control I would have until I became incapacitated. What I didn't know was how well everyone would work together, if they would respect my wishes, and if Nathan would bear the stress, even with Stephen and Susan helping.

But what if I didn't go to Stamford or to the nearest hospital on the Cape? That left two alternatives: let my body kill itself, which would be excruciating without sophisticated pain management, or kill my body. I couldn't do the first—not to myself or to Stephen.

Coming unsteadily to my feet, I tried to straighten without much success. I groaned and slowly made my way into the living room where Stephen was reading a yellowing paperback. He laid it on the table and looked at me expectantly.

"Dinner is ready whenever you are."

I shook my head. "I can only eat a little."

"That's okay, Bess. How's the fever?"

"Slightly better." I started to suggest that I look for a thermometer but what was the point? I lowered myself into an armchair, my body angled obliquely, the way I'd sat when pregnant with Nathan.

"And everything else?"

"Worse. Except my headache isn't as bad."

Stephen observed me with care. "So, have you figured things out?"

I rested my elbow on the chair's arm, propped my head on my hand, and stared at Stephen. "I know what I don't want to do."

"Which is?"

"I don't want to remain in this house, even if you stay with me."

"Are you sure?"

"Yes."

"Well, I agree."

I sighed and closed my eyes. "And I don't want to be admitted to the hospital and endure a series of operations that won't make any difference to the final outcome."

"They could control the pain there," Stephen replied.

"Yes, they could. But at what cost? To have my body and mind diminish each day? Lose my strength, independence, and who I am? Do I want Nathan to remember me in that final unrecognizable form, a body devoid of personality, incapable of expressing love?" I crossed my arms tightly across my chest. "No."

Stephen was silent, waiting. He already knew what I was going to propose.

20

"Let's eat and we can talk more," I suggested.

Stephen came to his feet, touched my shoulder, and left. After I fetched another oxycodone, I returned to the living room and sat at the table. The silverware and napkins had been neatly set. I heard the microwave door shut and a few minutes later the beep. This was repeated for the second meal. Stephen walked in from the kitchen, carrying two plates, one of which he placed before me. I stared at the food with revulsion, though I tried my best to disguise my reaction.

"Not exactly lobster, is it?" he said, pulling out his chair.

"No, but actually I'm glad it isn't." I lifted my fork with reluctance and speared a small piece of chicken. "Thank you for preparing it."

Stephen's plate was piled high. He ate swiftly, as if to remove the food from my sight. Between my few bites and his dispatch, our simple meal was over in minutes. After he patted his lips with a napkin, he gazed at me. His tranquility spread between us, a serenity that I welcomed but couldn't fully integrate. I was too upset, too full of conflicting emotions that were thrashing me raw.

I pushed away from the table. "Stephen, I can't go home. I can't go to the nearest hospital." My voice was weak, reflecting my exhaustion. "And I can't stay here much longer."

"Okay," he said quietly, "what can you do?"

"Tomorrow." I didn't explain what I meant.

Stephen understood.

—

After dinner, I switched on my phone and saw a message. Nathan had arrived in Stamford and was about to sit down with Hugh to eat Pasta Bolognese, one of my husband's specialties. I hoped they would talk and that Hugh would listen and demonstrate how much he loved his son.

I changed into my nightgown and crawled into bed. The night should have been made memorable, but I was too ill. Stephen and I watched television, a program I followed imperfectly due to the haziness induced by the opiates and the tumultuous thoughts whirling in my mind, thoughts which refused to cohere and settle. Stephen rubbed my back for a while, trying to ease the aching discomfort. The heat of his hand and the motion felt good, as he chased the pain in circles, but when he stopped, there was no lasting improvement. Soon after, the rice and chicken came up, and I spent a long time in the bathroom, emptying my stomach. When I was done, I glanced at my face in the mirror and saw that the yellow tinge was darker. My urine had also been dark, which I knew was another symptom of the bile blockage.

—

The next hours were a nightmare even with the fentanyl and the oxycodone. I felt like I was on an unstable ship, plunging downward into deep troughs of pain and clawing upward onto towering crests, hanging in momentary suspension. When I closed my eyes, the blackness seemed to split open with yellow lightning. Fever assaulted me; nausea ebbed and flowed. Not wishing to disturb Stephen, who was exhausted after two semi-sleepless nights with Nathan, I slipped out of bed and went into the guest room, lying down on Nathan's bed. The tears that hadn't come during the afternoon now fell freely, as I realized a line had been crossed between living versus spending most of my waking hours trying to stay alive and managing the rising pain. With this shift, my body would revert to the care of doctors, nurses, hospice aides, Susan, Nathan, and Stephen. But I was still responsible and would not cede that responsibility, that tremendous burden, to others. This awareness helped steady my vacillating emotions. I focused on my breathing, trying to slow and deepen respiration until I drifted into an uneasy slumber.

About 4:00 a.m., I woke and felt terrible. I returned to the master bedroom, reached for my laptop, and re-read the three letters, editing them modestly. In Hugh's note, I told him to stay in the house.

After transferring each into emails, I sent them into cyberspace, knowing they would devastate the three recipients. During this process, Stephen rose, braced himself against the pillows, and watched until I had powered down the computer. At my request, he replaced the older fentanyl patch on my back, and I took another pill. Knowing I couldn't eat, Stephen left to make himself breakfast. Slowly, I walked into the bathroom to look in the mirror, to confirm how sick I was. The yellow face in the glass made me recoil in horror. This was a stranger I scarcely recognized. I was now the cancer.

I dressed and packed my clothes, watch, bracelet, wedding band, phone, laptop, book, and purse in my suitcase. Stephen entered the room and, upon seeing what I'd chosen to wear, dressed accordingly. He removed his things from the closet and filled his bag, then went to run the dishwasher. After grabbing two prescription containers, I joined him and retrieved a bottle of water from the refrigerator, handing it to Stephen, who explained that he had already cleaned the kitchen and the house.

By the Dutch door, the room smelled of smoke and beach plum and old books. The cottage still retained some charm but that had faded as had my interest in my surroundings, in all things that had previously given me pleasure. At least this house was easier to leave than my home would be. And now it was time. I felt neither the urge to hurry or to procrastinate.

Outside, a wet sheen of dew covered the white car and its

windows. The dampness was heavy, befittingly somber, without the play of sunlight buffing the tiny drops into beads of gold. I shivered with an unexpected chill as the cool air struck my hot, feverish skin. The sky's black expanse was scattered with silver stars that were disappearing as the sun considered its eventual arrival. Unfortunately, I had missed the moon, which made me sad. And the owl that had been hooting nearby was now silent; no birds called from the trees, though I listened closely.

We walked to the car and Stephen placed our suitcases in the trunk. As I sat in the passenger's seat and closed the door, I remembered trips with my parents when we would begin journeys at this time; the early hour always seemed to intensify the excitement. My father would finish loading our luggage and join my mother in the front while I sprawled across the back seat propped against a pillow, my legs covered by a wool blanket. On the floor well opposite, I would usually place my brown leather briefcase stuffed with books, a deck of blue-and-white Bicycle cards wrapped with a rubber band, a diary to record my thoughts, and packs of my favorite Black Jack gum. I recalled how we would drive up steep mountains in Vermont and New Hampshire, and I would chew the gum so my ears would pop, a sensation that delighted me. In those days, people departed pre-dawn for vacations, and now I had risen at this hour once again and was setting off with Stephen.

Despite his imposing presence, I felt curiously alone. My body seemed to resonate like a hollow chamber, and, similar to those drives through mountains or during flights on airplanes as they ascended after takeoff, pressure filled my ears. The sound of the car's engine was muffled, distant. My vision seemed clouded or perhaps it was the ground fog that collected in the pockets between the dunes and hills, a silent whiteness that dropped its scrim over the emerald greens of bayberry and holly and the scarlet leaves of poison ivy, which were turning their autumnal color. We negotiated the drive and entered the road, passing through a dense curtain of mist. As the car nosed its way onto higher ground, the windshield wipers sweeping intermittently, the landscape clarified, though the taller trees were wreathed in fog as if sections had been erased. I thought of *Brigadoon* and how its village appeared every century when the mist suddenly lifted.

Was I entering such a magical place? Would I become younger, resembling Stephen's portrait, or was I rushing headlong into an abbreviated future? I wished I could return to my college years and make different decisions. Not to marry Hugh, for one, and to reside by the sea, for another. The rest? I didn't regret much else. Certainly not having Nathan or pursuing my career. I pictured the faces of some of my favorite clients and felt gratified that many had found new strength and optimism. One by one, silently, I bade each of them well.

Stephen was quiet. He drove more slowly than the day before, as if to allow time for me to sift through my memories. In his white shirt and shorts, with his white hair and skin, he appeared ghost-like, with only a faint green reflection shining on his face from the dashboard lights.

When we arrived, the fog had lifted and the sky was tinged with a wash of pinkish-orange, the color radiating upward from the resolute line of the horizon. It would be a beautiful late August day. Couples would spread blankets on the beach, and rainbow-colored umbrellas would throw ovals of shade over lovers like Nathan and Stephen. There would be picnic lunches, laughter. Now, no cars were parked in the lot except ours. I sat still for a moment, eyes closed, while Stephen circled around to open my door. If I didn't move, if I couldn't see anything, then perhaps I could pretend to be somewhere else and to be someone else.

I opened my eyes. Stephen was holding out his hand for mine. I took it and stepped out of the car, remembering when Hugh offered his hand after our wedding to help me into the limo, and, two years later, when he lowered baby Nathan into my arms as we departed from the hospital. Both times I was ecstatic and yet fearful of the responsibility, first of being a wife, then a mother. Those poignant emotions—all feelings—now seemed like vaporous contrails that were rapidly disappearing. I felt strangely flat, disassociated from the world and all the people in it.

Stephen placed his arm around me, and we trudged up the steep dune, one I'd climbed with relative ease on my second day on the Cape. Halfway to the top, my breathing was labored, my legs trembled, and my back radiated with pain. When we finally arrived at the summit, the sea air greeted me, fresh and cool from the embrace of night. I felt a small renewal of purpose.

"It's a little cold," Stephen said.

"It is."

These were the first words we'd spoken since we left the cottage. I hadn't even directed Stephen where to drive. He knew. He was now my destined companion, our mutual contract tacitly understood. The two things I questioned were if meeting Stephen in Provincetown had somehow hastened my illness, if he possessed a supernatural ability to speed the cancer's growth in order to avoid a prolonged emotional and physical suffering, with the intention of bringing me to this moment. Or, with similar magical acuity, had he sensed the disease's onslaught and hurried to my side, prepared to assist, allowing me to select the where and when of my demise? All I knew was that Stephen, in some mysterious way, wasn't altogether real.

We descended downward and walked onto the wide beach. About thirty feet from the shoreline, he stopped, pulled the water bottle out of his pocket and gave it to me. He removed his shirt and shorts, folded them in a neat pile, placed them on the sand, and dug a hole in which he laid his wallet and the keys to the car and house. I uncapped the two prescription bottles, shook out three oxycodone tablets and six sleeping pills, hoping they wouldn't make me sick, and handed the containers to Stephen. He added them to the pile, smoothed the sand over the top, and stood before me in his white bathing trunks, waiting.

"Up to you, Bess." He was calm, his words tinged with sorrow.

I kept my eyes fixed on his as I slid the pills into my mouth and swallowed them with two large gulps of water. It would take twenty minutes for the effects to begin, a little longer for full impact. I kicked off my sandals, unbuttoned my blouse, and unzipped my shorts, revealing my one-piece, black suit. I tucked my clothes in a small plastic bag and placed it next to Stephen's shoes.

Hand in hand, we strolled toward the sea. The large dome of sky loomed above us, impressive and majestic. Ahead, the dark greenish-blue water twitched with occasional whitecaps; the surf was full-bodied but not frenzied. We waded into ankle-deep water, our feet sinking into the sand as white foam overlapped itself in curving arcs. We embraced.

"Are you ready?" he whispered, gazing down at me. His eyes were once again blue, reflecting the changing color of the sky as the sun tipped the horizon.

I didn't speak, having entered into a dreamlike state where no decisions were necessary. All I needed to do was accept the one I'd made yesterday, to allow the sea's magnetism to draw me toward the sun. Although my strength was poor, I was an experienced swimmer and hoped that I could accomplish this last distance, however long it might be.

In response, I disengaged from Stephen and stepped farther into the water, its coldness a shock against my fevered skin. Nevertheless, I continued without hesitation until the water reached my thighs. I stopped to splash my shoulders and face to help adjust to the temperature; Stephen followed and did the same. A small wave broke, which I jumped, but I dove headlong into the next incoming breaker. When I surfaced, Stephen was nearby, his white hair matted and his broad shoulders glistening. My beautiful, magnificent sea god. I smiled at him, turned, and headed away from the beach, dipping under waves and feeling their throbbing power as they rushed over me. Each time I rose again, I inhaled deeply, filling my lungs. The numbing effects of the chilly water, painkillers, and sleeping pills lessened the discomfort. Feeling stronger, I swam past the line where the waves formed and began a steady crawl. My old rhythmic stroke, honed during childhood and practiced as an adult, remained in my body's memory. I exalted in how my hands bit into the water, cupping it in my palms and drawing handfuls behind me. Stephen easily kept pace to my left, matching his speed to mine. For a while, I enjoyed the familiar precision, the way I sliced through the ocean, but eventually the exhilaration died. Sadly, I no longer possessed my youthful vitality, and the drugs were starting to occlude my brain and weaken my muscles. Dizziness swept over me. My vision blurred. I rested.

"How are you doing?" Stephen asked.

"Tired." I glanced at the land and noted that it was about a half mile away. "Three years ago, I used to swim twenty laps in an Olympic-size pool. Sometimes more."

"When you need help, ask."

I nodded and turned to stare at the sun. It was partially hidden by a narrow strip of lavender-hued stratus cloud lying above the horizon. As I watched, a burst of tangerine backlit the cloud, then the sun rose higher so that the cloud became the sun's emphasis. Now, shining freely, a golden path flashed across the water and struck my face. I felt the sun's warmth and aimed eastward with fresh inspiration. Beside me, Stephen fell into his effortless stroke. After another four hundred feet, I slowed. Sleepiness, combined with weariness, was overtaking me, yet I knew that I could still swim to the beach, that I hadn't gone far enough.

Determined, I set out once more until turning my neck became too difficult. I modified the crawl, keeping my head above water, which wasn't efficient, but I couldn't take in enough air otherwise. Soon, I also stopped kicking because the movement sapped too much energy. Relying on my arms, with my legs trailing behind me, I struggled onward until I needed to catch my breath and to restrain strands of hair that had come loose. As I began to reach for my barrette, my arm felt so heavy that I let it slide into the water. Seeing my plight, Stephen unsnapped the barrette and gathered my hair within its clasp. I nodded thanks, and, after a moment in which my resolute mind vied with my tired body, I began again.

The water was very deep. I shuddered to think of what lurked in the darkness below, such as the two sharks that had circled near

Stephen on the first day. Fear shot through me. Were those savage creatures nearby? Such an eerie coincidence that they should appear when we met, or were they allies of Stephen's? Emissaries of death or perhaps its means? In my rapidly deteriorating state, was I conflating death, sharks, and Stephen into a single entity? Was he my pale horse, my pale escort? I recalled the newspaper article about the woman who had drowned at this same place on a day Stephen may have been present. Had my swimmer served as her companion? And what about the fatal boating accident suffered by his first adopted parents and the stroke that had befallen his second adopted mother? Was Stephen an agent for them despite his young age? Were there other deaths he hadn't mentioned? People in foster families, friends, classmates, colleagues, lovers, and strangers who had died in his presence, perhaps with his mysterious assistance? When they met on Fire Island, did Stephen select Terry because he sensed Terry's illness before any symptoms appeared? With the intention of easing the dying man's progress to the final ending, helping him as he was now helping me? All that I knew about Stephen whirled together into a mélange of incomplete and hazy details. I didn't even know how old he was. What had he told me? That he was "timeless." Like death itself? These contemplations should have filled me with horror, but the drugs were dulling the dread I had felt a moment ago. Stephen's identity didn't matter, I thought. Nothing did.

I kept swimming, on and on, fighting the exhaustion that had insinuated itself in my muscles, impeding their movement and my coordination. When I was too weak to continue, I slowed and turned over on my back, staying afloat by paddling. The sky was now an emphatic blue, sure of its color for the day to come. How many more minutes did I have to experience this beautiful world? I closed my eyes and kept moving my arms so that I wouldn't sink into the intense lethargy that was overcoming me. My respiration became shallower. My lungs felt lazy, like billows gone flat.

Stephen moved closer. "Bess, how much farther can you swim?"

I opened my eyes. His handsome face fluctuated from clear and sharp to gauzy and out of focus. Was Stephen really there beside me or was I alone in this vast ocean?

"Bess?"

"Yes?"

"How much farther?" Briefly, he glanced at the beach, then turned to me. "I think we're still too close."

"I'm so sleepy, Stephen," I murmured.

"I know." He circled around behind me, placed my head on his shoulder, and reached his left arm diagonally across my chest, pinning his hand under my arm and placing his body part-way under mine. This swimmer's carry allowed him to kick his legs and use his free right arm to do a sidestroke. I wanted to assist but I couldn't.

As we traveled onward, I thought about my mother and father. I didn't believe in heaven or reincarnation, yet I wasn't positive that we totally cease to exist after death. Perhaps our spirit lived on in some form, though I'd never seen any evidence that supported this idea—no ghosts or peculiar happenings. In the hospital, a few days before my father's passing, he promised he would always be with me. In the spring, he said, purple hyacinths would bloom in the front yard by the gray stone wall, as a sign that he was near. They did, but even at age ten, I knew the flowers came up there every year. Even so, I sat by the aromatic purple blossoms and felt a deep connection with him.

Soon enough I would know the answer to this greatest of all mysteries. Soon enough I might be reunited with my parents if their spirits had survived. Of course, there could be nothing, simply nothing. A void, an immense blackness, an infinite absence that is forever.

And Nathan? I regretted leaving him most. Would he blame me for what I was doing? Or would he understand that I was saving him from a terrible experience? Taking the responsibility for my life so that he wouldn't need to make painful choices or battle with conflicting impulses to stay or to flee? Giving him the ultimate gift that I could ever give? I wanted his last memory to be of me sitting on the patio, in the late afternoon sun, wine glass in hand, smiling.

Stephen was breathing heavily because of the awkward motion and the strain of advancing us through the oncoming waves. Finally, I told him to stop. He drew me against him and we floated. My head fell against his neck, and he pressed his cold lips to mine.

"Thank you," I whispered.

"It's my life's work," he murmured.

His life's work was tending to the dying. I tried to smile at this but couldn't muster the energy.

"Please, Stephen, when you tell Nathan…be gentle with him." There was more that I should say, yet as I stared at the sky, the words miraculously transformed into a flock of white birds. They spun in a graceful circle, gathered into an arrow, and flew toward the sun. Did it matter that I couldn't speak? Throughout my life I'd said enough, hadn't I?

My strength was gone. There was nothing to worry about. Stephen would ship my possessions to Stamford, drop off the keys to the cottage, and telephone Nathan rather than face him in person. Death had other plans, for other people.

"Let go, Bess," Stephen said in a low, tender voice. I looked into his eyes and saw no regret or hesitation, only sadness. "Let go. It's your time." Disengaging his arms, he edged away but continued to hold my hand.

Slowly, I slipped below the surface, yet remained anchored to Stephen. Pulling on his hand, I rose to take a small breath of air but sank again, this time inhaling seawater. It seemed fine to do this, natural, an acquiescence to my new domain. I felt Stephen release his grasp, his fingers trailing away from mine. I descended deeper. The blue sky and Stephen vanished. Shafts of golden light pierced the green water, and bubbles issued forth from my lips and journeyed upward in curling tentacles. My ears filled with the ocean's music, and the pain disappeared, ebbing away with all physical sensation. A sublime contentment pervaded my being. I was no longer a wife, mother, therapist; I was only myself and I was limitless.

With joy, I extended my arms and surrendered to the ocean.

ACKNOWLEDGMENTS

I am extremely grateful to Naomi Rosenblatt at Heliotrope Books, who has been an enthusiastic partner during the publication of this book, offering insightful editorial ideas and invaluable collaboration on the design and production. The novel's original developmental editor, Dr. Helga Schier, provided brilliant suggestions, and my dear friend and copy editor, Beverly Jean Harris, smoothed over rough patches in the manuscript and saved me from some errors. I also wish to thank my wonderful readers: Pat Barker Cooper, Carol Oberle, and Dr. Dwight Wilson, as well as my supportive friends, Julie and Tom Stewart, Karla Linn Merrifield, Shari Friedman, Jane Rundell, and colleagues from my days at Princeton University Press. Huge thanks go to Vicki DeVico for her clever technical help on the cover and for my author's portrait. The cover photograph was taken by the talented Angela Previte, who rose numerous times before dawn to capture the sunrise at the beach.

The book is dedicated to Ruth Evelyn Stagg, in memory, and to all those suffering from terminal illnesses.

Photo by Vicki DeVico

ABOUT THE AUTHOR

Laury A. Egan is the author of *The Outcast Oracle*; a collection, *Fog and Other Stories*; a psychological suspense novel, *Jenny Kidd*; two mystery/romance titles, *A Bittersweet Tale* and *The Ungodly Hour*; and a comedy, *Fabulous! An Opera Buffa*. Her poetry volumes include *Presence & Absence*; *The Sea & Beyond*; *Beneath the Lion's Paw*; and *Snow, Shadows, a Stranger*. She lives on the northern coast of New Jersey. Website: www. lauryaegan.com

www.ingramcontent.com/pod-product-compliance
Lightning Source LLC
Chambersburg PA
CBHW051510260626
47162CB00008B/2905